SILVER SHOES

FOR ANDREA —
SO NICE MEETING YOU!
Love and light!
Enjoy the ride!
Best wishes always,
Paul Melodchein
OZTOBERFEST 2017

SILVER SHOES

a novel by

Paul Miles Schneider

REVISED EDITION

Silver Shoes

For more information on Paul Miles Schneider and his books, please visit: www.paulmilesschneider.com

For more information about the Oz books and L. Frank Baum, visit the International Wizard of Oz Club at: www.ozclub.org.

ISBN-10: 1515333876
ISBN-13: 978-1515333876

For Mom and Dad, who always believed.

With deepest love, admiration, and appreciation.

AUTHOR'S NOTE

Telling the tale. That's what is most important to me. I've also gussied up the writing a bit—smoothing out language, correcting minor errors, and refining prose here and there in my never-ending quest to make this as good as possible, given my abilities as a mere mortal and self-published author.

This is the definitive edition of *"Silver Shoes."* Call it the "director's cut," if you will, and if you already own a first edition, I am by no means advocating that you upgrade to this new model. However, if you haven't yet taken the journey with Donald Gardner, or if you prefer things new and improved, this is the ideal mode of transportation.

I'm proud of this story, and that is why I'm compelled to share it with as many people as possible. That's why I strive and struggle to make it better. *"Silver Shoes"* was first published in 2009 and was recognized as a Kansas Notable Book in 2010 by the Kansas Center for the Book and the State Library of Kansas. Its sequel, *"The Powder of Life,"* was published in 2012.

I am fast at work on a third novel in the series.

Until then ... enjoy the ride.

Best wishes always,

Paul

"Good gracious!" she cried.

For she was sitting on the broad Kansas prairie, and just before her was the new farmhouse Uncle Henry built after the cyclone had carried away the old one. Uncle Henry was milking the cows in the barnyard, and Toto had jumped out of her arms and was running toward the barn, barking furiously.

Dorothy stood up and found she was in her stocking-feet. For the Silver Shoes had fallen off in her flight through the air, and were lost forever in the desert.

— *L. Frank Baum*
"The Wonderful Wizard of Oz," 1900

Prologue

GEORGE CLARKE GRABBED hold of the metal latch and gave it a quick, forceful tug to the right, sliding the heavy barn door open a bit. As he wandered into the darkness, the expected musty smell of old wood and dust filled the air, mixed with the thick sweetness of fresh cut hay. He yawned absentmindedly, having been through this ritual a million times—or at least it felt that way to him. He could pitch hay, gather eggs, and clean the entire barn in his sleep if he had to. Sometimes, it felt like he did just that before heading off to school in the center of town.

Daily chores were a part of life on the farm, but he'd gotten used to them. They were as inevitable as the sun coming up and had made him physically strong and disciplined—that's what his parents told him, at any rate. Other ten-year-olds on the neighboring farms had to do them as well, so there was little point in complaining about them.

The air was chilly this particular morning, with a light mist hanging over the distant fields, almost like soft, gray snow.

Funny weather for a summer in Missouri, he thought.

George actually shivered as he reached with blind precision for the wooden pitchfork propped up in its usual place against a nearby post. He struggled to stay balanced, and it occurred to him that he was exhausted. He even went to bed early the night before, right after an exciting episode of *The Lone Ranger*. It was his favorite radio program along with *Sky King,* and he never missed either one. When it was over, he put his official cap gun holster and cowboy hat on the chair next to his bed, and he fell asleep as soon as he finished his prayers. But the strange noises started not long after that. Scratching sounds ... from just outside his window.

Probably a stray dog.

Hopefully it wasn't a fox or, worse yet—a coyote! At least none of the chickens had gone missing. He'd counted them earlier to make sure. His father was out in the alfalfa field already, hooking up the plow. George would have heard by now if any mischief had been found.

Whatever it was, it kept him awake most of the night, and he was paying a heavy price for it today.

As he shoved the pitchfork into a nearby pile of hay, his stomach growled. The tantalizing aroma of his mother's fresh, hot biscuits drifted into the barn to keep him company, reminding him of the tasty reward that lay ahead for a vigorous morning's work.

Then, without warning, George heard a noise.

He jumped back as a jolt of fear ripped through him. His heart was pounding in his chest.

It was a loud flapping sound, like an old canvas sail thrashing in a violent wind. It came from above his head, hidden high up in the rafters directly over him. George strained his eyes, squinting into the shadows, but it was no use. He stumbled a bit, trying to get out of the way, not knowing what to expect next.

"The barn is empty," he thought to himself with determination.

But it wasn't.

There was something else in there with him.

As his mind raced through the possibilities, he went over to the heavy door and dragged it open wider to see if he could get a good look at the intruder.

No luck. A dense layer of clouds blocked the morning sunlight, and he could barely make out the massive oak beams looming overhead.

Just then the barn let out an unsettling groan, like the great, creaking hull of a wooden ship. And without thinking of the consequences, George shouted into the darkness.

"Who is it? Who's up there?"

His voice sounded helpless and peculiar to him, and it cracked in fear of a response.

There was no answer at first.

Then something that was not human began to speak to him.

George bolted up in his bed with a loud gasp. He struggled to catch his breath. Cold sweat trickled down his forehead as he started to tremble.

The digital clock next to him read 2:26 AM.

It was only a *dream,* he realized.

Only a dream.

He repeated this reassuring thought over and over again in his mind for the next several minutes. Eventually he was able to calm himself down.

Why were these childhood memories coming back to haunt him?

Fifty-two years had passed—more than half a century since that first frightening moment of discovery in the barn.

A moment that had changed his life forever.

He could only guess that this was a warning sign. Something was coming now.

Who or *what* ... he didn't know.

"I'm too old for this," he thought out loud in desperation. His voice was ragged and drained from years of running. Years of fighting to survive and of staying one step ahead.

But they were zeroing in on him again. It wouldn't be long now. He was sure of it.

Chapter One

DONALD GARDNER WAS bored as he gazed out of the backseat window of the speeding car. Nothing but endless, flat, straight highway. The white dashed line pulsated, flickered, and escaped down the middle of the long road behind them as they drove. His thoughts began to wander with it.

This hadn't felt like a vacation to him.

"We'll have a wonderful time in Kansas," he could still hear his mother saying, a bit too cheerfully, right before they pulled out of the driveway.

She kept telling Donald and his father—sometimes with very little patience left in her voice—that they were going to have *fun* on this trip. After the first couple of days, she finally stopped mentioning it. And even if his cousins and aunts and uncles had managed to be somewhat "fun," Donald was hoping for a more exciting way to spend these last precious days of summer.

It was not meant to be.

Sitting in front of their giant TV—watching sports, game shows, and really bad home movies—and hearing all about how much he'd grown ... even going down to the "crick" at the end of the next block to catch "crawdads" ... had each worn out their welcome soon enough.

They were nearly home again now, and at least he'd have his own bed and shower back. He was grateful for that. His Uncle Rick and Aunt Jenny's shower creeped him out, with the white shag carpet on the bathroom floor and the turquoise dolphins and pink flamingos painted on the tiles.

His very own backyard and driveway would be waiting for him, too, for a few final end-of-season games with his best friends Jon Foster and Chris Bryant. This would be his one last hurrah with them, since, in a little more than two weeks, Donald and his buddies would be right back in school again.

He shivered at the thought.

It felt like it was only yesterday that he was saying good-bye to most of his classmates for the start of another summer filled with the infinite possibility of high adventure. *Nothing* could beat that feeling, and nothing could hope to measure up to it either. All the roads of the world were stretched out in front of him, each one calling to him on those first few days. Instead, looking back on it now, his summer had turned out to be ordinary—even dull. Sure, he enjoyed going to the swimming pool nearly every day with Jon and Chris, but that wasn't special.

And Donald had longed for this summer to be special.

At least nothing terrible had happened, he reasoned. But when his mom and dad told him he'd be coming along with them for an "exciting" road trip through Kansas, he had openly cringed. He even tried to get out of it several times, but he dropped that idea after a long, painful lecture from his dad. As it turned out, this was the most attention he received from his father all summer.

In a way, Donald had enjoyed this trip. At least he'd gone *somewhere.* He packed a suitcase, said so long to his friends, left his home, his neighborhood, even his own state, and traveled someplace new. His family didn't take many trips together—not like Chris, who traveled everywhere with his family. The Bryants had been abroad every summer ever since Donald could remember: Greece, Italy, Mexico, Germany, France, China … and now, this summer, Bermuda.

But it never seemed like there was enough time for the Gardners to get away like that. Plenty of business trips for each of his parents, though. Maybe for them that was adventure enough.

No matter.

They were heading home now, and next week Donald would be out shopping for school supplies with his mother, looking for new fall and winter clothes that would fit him better. And new shoes. And soon he'd have nine more months of memorizing historic dates, spelling words, and times tables.

This year, he would be in the sixth grade. That was going to be a kick! Donald would be one of the mighty *kings* of King Elementary School. He and his fellow classmates were at long last "the big kids on the block," and it felt really good. He was looking forward to it.

But something inside was tugging at him, perhaps letting him know this was his one last year of being a kid before heading off to junior high, bigger responsibilities ... and growing up.

As they zoomed along the road, the dull Kansas landscape seemed to repeat itself in an endless cycle.

Donald's eyelids grew heavier, and he had almost fallen asleep when he realized their car was slowing down.

His father was pulling off the road.

"We need to make a quick stop, Donny," he announced. "Hope we aren't disturbing you back there."

The boy sat up for a moment and looked around. He was surprised his father was even speaking to him. For some reason, that idea amused him a bit, too.

"No ... I just thought maybe we were home already," he replied, followed by a sizeable yawn.

He made the decision right then not to show any unnecessary enthusiasm over his dad's sudden interest in him.

"We got a million miles to go, kid," said Mr. Gardner, then he laughed. "You oughta get out and stretch your legs. Do you need to go to the bathroom?"

Donald rubbed the sleep from his eyes. "I'm okay," he answered. "Where are we?"

"Beats me," said his father with a slight jab in his voice. Then he shrugged, glancing over at Donald's mother sitting next to him, and gave her a teasing grin.

"Don't start that again," she said. "We're still in *Kansas,* if that's what you mean."

"Anybody want a Coke?" offered Mr. Gardner, skillfully changing the subject.

"I do!" shouted Donald, as if the mere mention of an ice-cold beverage could bring him miraculously back to life.

"Me, too," added his mom. "Anything diet."

"Why don't you both wait by the car and stretch a bit?" said his father. "And don't wander off anywhere. We need to hit the road again soon if we're going to make it home at a decent hour."

Then he left the two of them alone and went inside the store.

Mrs. Gardner got out first, followed by Donald, who stepped out of their black SUV and began to look around.

There wasn't the slightest temptation to wander off anywhere. The sun was already turning a deep, rosy red with long, curved, purplish streaks in it.

"Kansas has awesome sunsets," he thought to himself. "At least it's good for that."

He could smell the sweet grass, too. Kentucky bluegrass. That's what his mom told him it was. The agreeable fragrance caught hold of a light breeze and made its way through the warm, muggy air.

They had pulled off the main road onto a widened, graveled shoulder. Not much to look at: a filling station and a rundown, mom-and-pop store where his newly observant father was, at this moment, buying Cokes all around; a tall, faded sign on a splintery post next to the road with the words "Gas, Food, Drink" in red-and-black chipped letters; a dusty travel trailer hitched to an even *dustier* pickup truck parked under the sign ....

As Donald stretched and yawned, he realized there wasn't a single building on the horizon—just the open road spreading out in both directions, with more dirt, gravel, and shrubs along the way. He counted a few trees here and there, but not many.

"Excuse me," said a voice from under the signpost.

Donald was caught off-guard and turned to find a woman standing in the doorway of the travel trailer.

She was poor. He could tell right away from her clothes. She wasn't old either, not like his grandma was. He figured she was closer to his mom's age. She had stringy, light-brown hair that hung down in her face and needed a good shampooing, he decided. Her blue canvas sneakers were dirty and threadbare with tiny holes and rips along the sides and over the toes. She wore a faded cotton dress with little flowers sewn into it. Donald guessed she didn't have many others.

"I hope I'm not botherin' you nice people," the woman added with a faint smile.

"Not at all," his mother replied, and from the waver in her voice, Donald sensed she was feeling uneasy and even a bit saddened by this woman. "We just stopped here for a minute. We're on our way home."

The woman looked nervous and hesitated, but then she stepped down out of the trailer and started toward them. She was holding something large and metallic in her hands. It flashed with brilliant reflections in the rays of the setting sun.

"I wonder if you might be interested in this," she announced as she held her shiny object out for both of them to see. There was a telling hint of excitement in her voice as she approached. She glanced around at the same time, almost as if to make sure no one else was watching her.

Donald's mother started to turn away. He had seen her do this before with strangers who were trying to sell her something. It was an impulsive, cautious reaction that he didn't quite understand. She brushed a strand of long, reddish-brown hair out of her eyes and started to say something to the woman like, "We're not interested in buying anything today, lady," but then she stopped herself. She relaxed her shoulders instead and turned back again. She appeared to be having a change of heart. This woman was clearly not a threat to them.

Mrs. Gardner gazed at the object, focusing her full attention on it.

Could it be a piece of silver?

It looked genuine enough to Donald, although he was no expert. His mom collected antique silver, though, and had done so ever since she was a little girl.

As the woman came closer, he could see now that it was some sort of shoe.

"Unusual, ain't it?" she remarked in an anxious, whispered tone. Obviously, she was trying to impress them, but it was clear to Donald that this was awkward for her.

"It's silver, isn't it?" his mother inquired with a good-natured grin.

"Oh, you bet," she replied in eager haste. "I just *knew* it when I saw you two standin' there. You were the folks to appreciate it. My great-granddaddy found this, one day, out in a field not far from here—over a hundred years ago, so they tell me."

Her shoe was oddly shaped with strange, decorative carvings all over it. It reminded Donald of a Dutch wooden clog mixed with something out of *The Arabian Nights*. It even looked large enough to wear.

"It was his prize possession," the woman added, and she raised it up higher to give them a better look. "From the day he found it, he never let nobody else in our family touch it, nor come anywheres near it. He was convinced it was worth a lot of money and that someday he might have to sell it if they ever got into any financial trouble. I guess he was mighty thankful that day never did come," she said. Then she lowered her eyes and continued in a softer voice. "After a while, it got passed on to my granddad, then on to Daddy. Then he give it to me, swearin' me to secrecy. Each of us kept it hid. Didn't want nobody to even know about it. But the day has come for me now when—"

She paused and swallowed hard.

"I need to part with it," she finished after a moment.

She glanced back at the trailer, and for the first time, Donald sensed she might be afraid.

"Are you sure you want to sell it?" his mother asked.

"Ma'am, I got to. It's the only way," she replied. "Now what d'ya say? How much you give me for it?"

Donald's mother stared at the woman with concern, then back at the impressive shoe as she stood thinking.

"Please, ma'am, how much?" tried the woman again with more urgency this time.

His mother pondered a bit longer, then nodded.

She opened the car's front passenger door, leaned in, and pulled out her purse. Then she began to shuffle through it.

"Let's see," she replied. "I've got a hundred and twenty ... no, wait ... a hundred and *sixty* dollars cash."

"Mom?" interrupted Donald.

"Haven't you got more'n that, ma'am?" said the woman who was now clearly pressed for time.

"Look, why don't you try selling it at an auction or on the Internet?" said Mrs. Gardner. "You could get it appraised first, and—"

"I can't do that, ma'am. I gotta sell this now and be on my way. Is there anything else you got?"

"You didn't *steal* it, did you?" the boy said without warning.

"Donald!" his mother cut in quickly. She paused with an embarrassed smile. "Look, I *am* sorry, and I apologize for my son's behavior now—but as rude as that might have sounded, he has a good point. I must admit the thought crossed my own mind."

"I don't blame you for thinkin' it, ma'am, but, as God is my witness, I didn't steal it. It's just like I told you, I swear."

Mrs. Gardner looked at the shoe again. "I don't even know if it's real silver," she remarked out loud. "Well—*one* of us is getting ripped off," she added with a chuckle in an unsuccessful attempt to ease the tension between them. Then she held out her folded-up bills and shrugged. "I'm sorry, but this is all I can offer you. One hundred and sixty dollars."

The woman stared at the money. Donald thought she might actually cry. She straightened up after that, took a deep breath, and surrendered her most valued treasure.

"I gotta take your money, ma'am, and I thank you for your offer."

She pocketed the cash, following a quick handshake as if to seal the deal, then walked with great determination back to her trailer. She hesitated and turned at the door.

"God be with you both," she added with a raised hand.

"Good luck to you, too," said his mother.

On impulse, Donald waved at the woman, then watched with curious fascination as she went inside her trailer again and closed the door.

He wondered where she was going. She definitely needed that money.

Maybe she was running away.

"I must be out of my mind," Mrs. Gardner muttered to herself as she slipped the shoe into her travel bag. "Please promise me you won't say a word about this to your father," she added with a sigh, touching Donald's shoulder. "You know how angry he gets about stuff like this—and I definitely don't need to hear a lecture on the way home tonight."

Donald smiled. "I like the shoe, Mom, even if it's a fake. It's pretty cool. He doesn't need to know."

She reached over and smoothed his messy brown hair.

"I realize this hasn't been the best vacation for you, kiddo," she said with quiet understanding. "You've been a good sport about everything, though."

Donald gave her a faint grin, then gazed at the sky again.

"Every summer's the same," he said. "I always hope something awesome will happen ... but it never does."

"One day, you'll see. We'll all go someplace terrific and have a big adventure together."

Donald nodded. "That would be awesome."

"As for your father," she continued, "he tries his best, but he's a busy man with a lot on his mind. And sometimes it might seem like—"

"You don't have to say it, Mom. It's okay," he interrupted softly. "It's not a big deal."

Just then Mr. Gardner came out of the store carrying an overstuffed paper bag.

"Did I miss anything?" he asked with his typical sarcasm.

"Not really," she replied. Then she looked down at her son who was staring off into the vast twilight sky.

Donald felt himself being pulled over the horizon and beyond ... to someplace unknown, someplace filled with possibilities ....

Someplace else.

He closed his eyes, then opened them again, realizing his mother was waiting for him to lend her a little support.

"Just a cool sunset, Dad," he added with a yawn.

His father reached into the bag and handed them each a can of cold soda as they climbed back into the car for the final leg of their journey home.

Chapter Two

DONALD WAS RELIEVED to discover that he had Mrs. Harper for sixth grade. She was the popular teacher. Miss Wallace, the other sixth grade teacher, was the mean one. And if that didn't make life sweet enough, his two best friends, Jon and Chris, were also going to be in his class. He breathed easier now, knowing everything was shaping up to be great for the fall.

Mrs. Harper had the reputation of being a little crazy—of course that all depended on who was doing the talking. Some of the older kids in the neighborhood said she was the best teacher they ever had, while a few of their parents called her "eccentric" or "unorthodox." She was always arguing with the principal and defending her teaching methods in front of the school board. At least that's what he heard.

He figured it would keep things *interesting,* at any rate.

From everything Donald could tell, Mrs. Harper seemed wonderful, and he counted himself lucky to be among her newest crop. He even gave her a happy grin on that first day as he walked into the classroom and took an available seat after reviewing the room assignments posted in the hall.

She peered back at him over her horn-rimmed reading glasses with a pleasingly crooked smile and sparkling, focused eyes. Then she continued to watch each of her new students file into the classroom for the first day of their final year of grade school.

Things were definitely looking up.

As the afternoon drew to an end, she gave them each a simple homework assignment to bring something new with them to school the next day, something they had either bought, found, or made during their summer vacation. They would share the object with the class as a way of getting to know each other better.

This couldn't have been a worse first assignment for Donald!

His summer had been one gigantic yawn, and now he was going to have to stand up in front of practically everyone he knew and tell them that his life was totally boring.

He thought about pretending to be sick. He could fake a stomach ache pretty well these days. Besides, what could he bring in that was remotely interesting?

His friend Jon had a new racing bike. He was always getting stuff like that. Jon's parents regularly rewarded him for winning a blue ribbon or collecting a trophy at a swim meet—or for coming in first in track or hitting the most home runs. That was an easy one. Jon Foster would show off his bike, no question.

And Chris had gone to Bermuda this year, returning with the coolest shark's tooth necklace. He could talk for days about all the amazing things the Bryant family did while they were off exploring the world together.

Then Donald thought about driving across dusty old Kansas with his parents.

"Oh, yeah, that'll really get them excited," he grumbled to himself with mock enthusiasm. "I'll be the coolest kid of all, hands down."

The most pathetic part was that he didn't have a thing to show for that week he spent in Boringville.

Then suddenly it hit him.

The shoe!

He'd kept his word with his mother about not bringing it up. In fact, he had almost forgotten about their roadside pit stop on the way home. He remembered seeing his mom slip the shoe into a cloth tote bag when everyone was running around unpacking from the trip. She had left the bag hanging in her bedroom closet.

As far as he knew, it would still be there.

She hadn't mentioned it once since putting it away and had likely forgotten it herself. At least he could tell his classmates about the strange lady who sold it to them for a hundred and sixty bucks.

It wasn't much of a story, he thought ... but it was the best he had to work with.

Summer Show-and-Tell began just after first bell the next morning, and one by one, Mrs. Harper asked each of her students to stand at the front of the room.

"These kids all have way more exciting lives," thought Donald to himself as he watched a parade of interesting objects, "and way cooler stuff, too."

He was glad about the shoe at least. He managed to smuggle it successfully out of the house, wrapped in a brown paper bag, without his mother so much as raising an eyebrow. He was such a skilled criminal, he decided with pride.

Eventually it was his turn to face the class.

"Donald, what have you brought for us today?" asked Mrs. Harper.

"Well ..." he responded.

And with that brief, verbal drum roll, he reached inside his crumpled bag and pulled out the mysterious-looking object, holding it up for his classmates to see. Some of the students let out an audible, "Ooooh," and he could tell that even Mrs. Harper was surprised by it. Jon and Chris looked back at him with dropped jaws.

"Where did you get *that?*" cracked Chris.

"Okay ..." began Donald with a fair amount of showmanship for a sixth-grader. "We were driving across Kansas from our vacation about two weeks ago when my dad decided to pull off the road and stop at this store."

He looked down at the shoe for a moment, then held it up again before he continued.

"My mom bought it off a weird lady who was there—for a hundred and sixty bucks. She said it might be real silver."

"That's a very unique shoe, Donald," Mrs. Harper remarked as she adjusted her disheveled, graying hair. "I can't decide whether it's ornamental or ceremonial."

She paused, staring at it with a fixed expression.

Donald looked around and saw he wasn't the only one confused by her words.

She tried again right away. "I'm sorry, class. I mean I can't tell if this shoe was intended for *decoration* or if it was to be *worn,* perhaps as part of a ceremony or festival. It certainly is unusual."

"A silver shoe," said one blonde girl who was new to the school. Donald didn't know her yet. "Just like in *The Wizard of Oz,*" she added.

Several students began to giggle.

"No, it isn't," he snapped. Then he shifted his feet from side to side as his anger began to rise. "Those shoes were *red*. Everybody knows that. They were made out of rubies."

"Not in the book," said Mrs. Harper, putting a damper on the dispute. "You've all read the original story, haven't you?"

A few scattered hands went up.

"Some of you are embarrassed to admit it, I see," she added with a sigh. "You shouldn't be. And if you *had* read it, you would know in the book by L. Frank Baum those magic shoes were made of *silver*. They were switched to Ruby Slippers for the movie, so they would look better in Technicolor. You see, color movies were still quite new in the 1930s, and the filmmakers wanted to take advantage of it and show off the bright red." She laughed. "I confess I've always been a huge fan of both the Oz books and the MGM film, so I guess I know *more* than my fair share on the subject. And Katie is right. It's not a bad observation either. Well done."

Donald felt defeated and embarrassed. His one cool summer event had been reduced to nothing more than fairy-tale kid stuff by this dumb new girl he didn't even know. His life was truly over, he thought.

"This isn't a *Wizard of Oz* shoe," he replied with insistence. "The woman who sold it to us said it was over a hundred years old."

"Mr. Baum wrote his novel more than a hundred years ago, Donald. Of course, it was *fiction,* and I don't mean for you to take Katie's observation as fact. But you shouldn't look so sour about it either. Those were wonderful stories full of merry adventures, great battles, fascinating characters, powerful magic, and some pretty scary stuff along the way. I suggest to anyone who hasn't read the Oz books, give them a chance sometime. You might be surprised at what you find. Now who's next?"

Donald returned to his seat trying hard not to feel bad about this.

He just knew Jon and Chris were going to lay into him big-time on his walk home from school, so he attempted to get a head start by sneaking out right after the bell.

They caught up with him soon enough as he crossed through the grassy field and started down the narrow sidewalk toward home.

"Hey, Donny, wait up!" said Chris, grinning from ear to ear. His large, white teeth were gleaming even brighter than usual, offset by his dark curly hair and the deep tan he was still sporting from his most recent island adventures. "What's up with that witch's shoe?"

"I can't believe your mom spent a hundred and sixty bucks on it," said Jon, sitting with imperious authority on his new bike. He was managing to look even taller and blonder these days.

Donald turned to face them both with a calm smile.

"She said if it's real silver, it's worth a lot more than that," he replied. "The woman was really weird. You guys had to be there."

"But what if it's *not* real silver?" said Jon, pedaling backwards as he shifted gears. "Then your mom got suckered, I guess."

"Hey, I got a better idea," said Chris. "What if it really is a *witch's* shoe?"

Jon roared with laughter and almost fell off his bike.

"Come on," said Donald with a groan.

"No, seriously," Chris continued, and he tried to stop Jon's obnoxious snorting with a judgmental glare. "It could have all sorts of cool powers if it was real, right?"

"Oh, yeah, *right,*" said Donald.

"Hey, let me see it again," said Jon, settling down a bit. His face was still red from laughing so hard.

"No way," said Donald. "You've had too much fun already."

He clutched his crumpled bag close to his chest, turned away, and started for home.

"I'm not kidding anymore," said Chris, trying again. "Look, I'm sorry for baggin' on you, Donny. I didn't get a good look at it in school, all right? It is kinda neat. Let's see it again."

"Come on, show it to us," said Jon. The color in his face had returned to normal at last.

Donald stopped.

"This is going back in my mom's closet," he said. "She hasn't told my dad about buying it yet, and she doesn't even know I took it to school today. All right?"

"We swear we won't touch it," said Jon.

"We just want to see it one last time," added Chris.

Donald knew the kidding had stopped. They had all been best buddies since kindergarten, and he felt he could trust them both with his life if he had to. So, after one final hesitation, he unrolled the paper bag and reached inside.

A moment later, they were staring at the remarkable shoe again.

"Where do you suppose it came from?" asked Jon.

"The lady who sold it to us said her great-grandfather found it in a wheat field," he replied. "Or something like that. Somewhere in Kansas. They kept it secret for over a hundred years."

"It doesn't look that old," said Chris. "Doesn't silver tarnish?"

"No scuff marks or dents or anything," said Jon. "Just those weird carvings and symbols on it. It looks brand new."

"It might be fake, then," said Chris.

"It probably wasn't ever worn," thought Donald out loud. "Maybe Mrs. Harper was right—it was just for decoration, not for wearing."

"It looks like you could wear it if you wanted to," said Chris. "It's big enough to fit a foot."

"Have you tried it on, Donny?" asked Jon, and he chuckled at the thought. "You've got tiny feet."

"Okay, *that's* it," he announced, opening his bag again.

If there was one thing he couldn't stand from either of them, it was being teased about his size. It was bad enough when it came from Chris, but Jon was a good five inches taller than him now.

"No, I haven't tried it on!" he continued. "Do you think I'm crazy? I don't go around wearing girls' shoes."

"What if it's got weird, magic powers?" said Chris, urging him further.

"I'm not putting it on."

"You could become *all-powerful in the universe,*" said Jon.

"It's a woman's shoe!" shouted Donald.

"It doesn't really *look* like a woman's shoe," said Chris.

"Well, it doesn't look like a man's shoe either," he replied.

"I dare you to put it on," said Jon, challenging him.

"Me, too," added Chris. "I *double-dare* you to try this on right now!"

Donald set his backpack down.

"Okay, look, if I try it on ... will you swear not to tell anybody and swear never to talk about it again?"

His friends looked at each other and shrugged.

"We swear," they replied in agreement.

"We just want to see if it actually fits," said Chris.

Donald glanced around to make sure no one else could be watching this.

The coast was clear.

Then he plopped down on the sidewalk, kicked off his left sneaker, and adjusted his white sock. He held the silver shoe out in front of him—and for a moment, time seemed to stop. He felt his thoughts drifting away, carrying him toward some unknown place.

For an instant, he was lost in the intricate, mysterious markings carved into the shoe's silvery surface. He began to trace his fingers lightly over them ...

... searching for ....

"Come on, hurry it up. Just give it a try," said Jon.

Then, all at once, the shoe was on his foot.

"Hey, it fits!" shouted Chris. "Can you stand up in it?"

Donald rose to his feet and stared at it, frowning. This shoe looked ridiculous to him. He shook his head in disapproval.

"Who would want to wear such a weird-looking—"

The words caught in his throat as he felt a small vibration stirring in his toes.

"Whoa ..." he whispered.

The sensation grew stronger, moving slowly up his left leg, followed by the overwhelming feeling of ... *despair*.

"What's the matter, Donny?" said Jon.

But he couldn't explain it. Donald was being pulled into a very cold, dark place—and before he could answer, the three boys gazed up at the sky.

The sun was dipping behind a group of oddly shaped clouds. Were they imagining this? The clouds began to fan out and spread across the horizon. It was now noticeably but uncomfortably *different* than it had been a moment earlier. The wind picked up around them as well, and Donald could hear it rustling through the tall grass in the empty field next to them. A few crisp leaves, the first of the season, crackled and circled around them in a bizarre, agitated dance.

Everything felt suddenly alive.

Then Donald came to his senses and found his voice again.

"I ... I don't know," he replied. "Something just happened."

The boys stood together in silence and did their best to grasp the subtle shift in their surroundings.

After a moment, Donald sat down again, slipped the silver shoe off, and placed it back in his crumpled bag.

His heart was pounding.

"Let's get out of here," said Chris. "Enough of this Voodoo."

"Yeah, I think we need to go home now," added Jon with a nervous nod.

Donald tied his sneaker up in record time, jumped to his feet, and started running down the sidewalk after them.

Chapter Three

AS HE LAY in his bed that night, staring up at the tiny bumps on his ceiling, Donald was glad this particular day was over. He breathed a sigh of relief, playing back the recent events in his mind. He had made it through Mrs. Harper's Summer Show-and-Tell and the minor humiliation that followed—and he decided to forgive that new girl Katie for her dumb *Wizard of Oz* comment. She didn't mean anything by it. Besides, he liked her smile and thought about striking up a conversation with her when he was sure no one was looking. He also survived Jon and Chris's jabs on the way home, and that strange, indescribable feeling when he tried the silver shoe on. It had taken him several hours plus the help of three mindless

TV shows to shake it off again. He even managed to smuggle the borrowed object back into his mother's closet without anyone noticing it was missing from its secret hiding place.

Mission accomplished! Game over.

He wondered if she would ever *do* anything with it or just leave it hanging in the closet, tucked away forever.

That didn't seem right.

He couldn't stop thinking about those weird carvings on the shoe's surface, either. He had never seen anything like them. One thing was certain—he knew his father would get really upset if he ever discovered how much she'd paid for it. This would not be the first time she traded a wad of cash for a piece of silver that turned out to be worthless. To her, it was like gambling in a casino. She would trust her instincts, close her big blue eyes, hand over her money, and pray really hard to win back a fortune. Donald liked that his mom *occasionally* took risks, though. It made life more interesting.

He woke up suddenly.

Moonlight filled the empty room.

There was a scratching sound—a faint noise coming from just outside his bedroom window. Donald tried to pretend it wasn't there at first. It was only the wind, or maybe he was dreaming ... or it was a tree branch scraping against the house.

Except no branches were close enough to touch his window.

He rubbed his eyes and waited as the room fell silent again. Then he forced the notion out of his mind and rolled over in his bed.

Donald had a vivid imagination, no doubt about it. He was always pretending to be *somewhere* or *someone* else. It was a talent he developed growing up as an only child—an easy way to entertain himself whenever he felt like it.

It also came in handy whenever he was scared. He could concentrate on other things and block out the entire world if he felt like it.

Lying in his bed now, he decided to play the game.

He would be a farmer's son this time, something he'd never tried before. Perhaps it was his recent road trip through Kansas inspiring him.

Donald was good at picturing details, too. He could see an enormous wooden barn out back behind the house. The images were vivid—even more so than usual—almost as if they were a memory instead of his imagination.

It was an early summer morning with a fine layer of mist, and he was busy with his daily chores like most kids on a farm would be at this hour. The weather was unseasonably cold, he decided. It made him shiver in his boots.

And this was a long time ago. Maybe fifty years or so. His clothes looked different than they do now.

He could smell hot biscuits baking inside the house. His mother was almost ready with his breakfast, and he was hungry, too. Donald had just finished gathering eggs from the henhouse, and he yawned, standing in front of the huge door, as he reached over to lift its heavy metal latch and slide it open.

Then he entered the chilly barn. He could barely see his own hand in front of him as he grabbed a pitchfork leaning against a post and plunged it deep into a pile of hay ...

... when, all at once, a loud flapping sound startled him from above.

Donald sat up in his bed and held his breath.

The scratching noise was right outside his window.

He didn't move.

He sat there for several minutes waiting to hear what would happen next.

Nothing followed.

After what seemed like an eternity, he gave up and lay back in his bed, staring up at the ceiling.

He tried to fall asleep again and felt curiously alone this time. It was an uncomfortable sensation, as if everyone else on the planet had vanished into thin air. He knew it wasn't true, of course, but he found himself fighting an overpowering impulse to sneak out of bed, tiptoe across the hall, and take a quick, confirming peek at his sleeping parents.

Instead, he remained snug under the covers and continued to mull over this bizarre notion. He almost laughed out loud at the ridiculousness of it. Then he recalled the old black-and-white *Twilight Zone* episode—the one where a husband and wife ran all around an empty town together, looking for other people or any signs of life. He remembered sneaking downstairs after hours one night to watch it, and he grinned with new appreciation of it. Jon and Chris would share a good laugh with him over this whole creepy scenario on their walk to school tomorrow.

Donald shook his head and breathed a deep, reassuring sigh. Then he scrunched down under the covers again and tried his best to relax.

Soon the strange engravings on the silver shoe reappeared in his thoughts. Their detailed shapes and well-crafted curves swirled and danced inside his mind, determined not to be forgotten. Each silvery likeness flared up, then burned crimson-red with its own lasting impression—like sunspots blooming before his eyes that refused to go away. Yet somehow, he knew these markings were important, although he couldn't understand why he thought so. He began to study them, detached from all emotion, as they floated in and out of his consciousness.

Then, without warning, he was overcome by the same feeling of *despair* that he'd felt earlier. There wasn't a thing he could do to stop it either. It was coursing through his veins with an icy vengeance.

There it was again! The noise at the window.

He was sure of it this time. This was no dream, and it was even more aggressive than before. He held the covers in his clenched fists and sat up in bed. It was a steady, gnawing, scratching sound, like a wild animal with huge claws or teeth.

It *must* be in his mind. He had worked himself into a frenzy thinking about that stupid shoe. There was no other explanation for it.

As logic continued to fail him, he glanced at the opposite wall. The pale moonlight cast an eerie sheen across the front of his dresser when suddenly he saw a shadow pass by the window.

His heart jumped into his throat.

The dark, unidentifiable shape grew larger and eclipsed the moonlight, followed by a low yelping sound, like a wounded animal caught in a hunter's trap. Then, almost as if he were watching an old silent movie flickering in slow-motion, he saw the window inch up in its frame.

Something was out there. *And it was trying to get into his room!*

Donald drew a deep breath and let out a scream.

Moments later, his mother stood in the doorway, gasping for air as she flipped the overhead light on.

"Donny, what is it?" she said, panting. "Are you okay?"

His father was right behind her as Donald choked through his response. "Something's outside! It's trying to get in here!"

Mr. Gardner crossed to the window and peered out into the night.

"What do you see?" said Donald with an unsteady voice.

"Why don't you have a look for yourself?" he answered after a few seconds.

Donald hesitated, then joined his dad.

The driveway below them was empty in the soft moonlight. Donald could see the familiar row of houses across the street. Most of them had their lights off now. The lamppost at the far end of the block flooded its corner with hazy pools of illumination.

Everything was peaceful and calm, just as it *should* be at this hour of the night.

Then Mr. Gardner pulled the window back down in its frame ... and locked it.

"Donny, there's nothing out there," he said.

"I swear I heard it," said Donald, who sat at the edge of his bed and started to cry.

"That must have been a pretty good nightmare," said his mother, scooting in next to him. "You scared the life out of us."

She stroked her son's head.

"No, Mom, it was trying to claw its way in here. It lifted the window up, and I could see a *shadow* outside. Then I heard the screeching. You must have heard it, too."

"I heard screeching, all right," said Mr. Gardner with a teasing grin, "but it was coming from *you*."

"Donny, look, there's nothing out there," said his mother, crossing to the window herself. "Just the moon. There isn't even a breeze tonight."

Donald was silent, lost in his confusion. He looked up at both of them after a moment and nodded in resignation. Then his mother sat on the edge of the bed again.

"Are you going to be okay, kiddo?" she asked.

"Yes," he replied, wiping his face with the back of his hand. "I guess I just had a bad dream."

She leaned over and kissed his forehead while she combed her fingers through his hair.

"No more sweets before you go to bed," she added with a smile.

"I'll be all right," he answered. Then he leaned back and rested his head against the pillow.

His father let out a disinterested yawned and walked out of the room—but his mother stayed a few minutes longer.

After she left him alone again, Donald discovered he was still very much afraid.

He knew, deep down in his heart, that it had not been a dream.

Morning came, and the sun was shining down on another day. Donald had almost forgotten about the disturbing incident from the night before.

Strange things often happen during the dark hours of the night, he reasoned.

Clearly, a nightmare was the answer—although, at the time, it seemed *so real* to him. This was the easy explanation, of course, but one he decided to live with.

After polishing off a bowl of cereal, he gave his mom a quick kiss on the cheek. She had let him sleep in, under these abnormal circumstances, and she informed the school's main office that her son would be running late. Jon and Chris went on without him, so Donald scooped up his backpack and headed for the door alone.

As he hurried along the sidewalk, passing the houses of his friends and neighbors, he thought once more about the ridiculous nightmare summoned out of his wild imagination.

A *howling monster* scratching at his window?

A burglar with supernatural powers able to break into a second-floor bedroom without the use of a ladder?

None of it made sense.

As he shook his head and laughed, a different but equally uncomfortable feeling surfaced.

Donald walked slower trying to identify it. He continued up the path toward his school—this time, with a little extra caution and awareness that something just didn't feel right.

Then suddenly it swept through him with an overpowering realization.

He was being watched.

He stood perfectly still as his heart started to race. It was broad daylight now, and everything was in plain view. He turned in a slow deliberate circle, scanning his surroundings down to the last detail. There wasn't anything out of place: the rows of familiar houses; the small rock wall running next to the sidewalk with the bare snapdragon bushes along the top of it; the same old cars parked in their usual spots. Nobody was around at this moment, but that wasn't out of the ordinary for this time of day. Most people were at work already or in school. Still, he couldn't shake the undeniable feeling that he wasn't alone.

After nearly a minute, Donald was able to dismiss it, and he started up the sidewalk again toward the open field in back of the school. He had almost reached the top of the hill, just a few houses away from the edge of the field, when he heard a branch snap.

He turned to his left to see where the noise was coming from. Out of the corner of his eye, he caught a glimpse of a lumbering, dark, horrible shape as it slipped silently behind the large trunk of an oak tree.

This was not a dream.

Panic flooded his mind as he dropped his backpack and began to sprint up the hill. He could see his school on the far side of the grassy field.

It was sanctuary.

He kept going as fast as he could until he arrived at the side entrance. He tore the door open with all his might and raced down the empty hallway. The pounding of his tennis shoes on the tile floor echoed off the brick walls. Then he stopped as he reached the doorway to his classroom.

Everyone reacted to the commotion—even Mrs. Harper, who broke off in the middle of a sentence. She peered over the rim of her glasses with a concerned look.

"Donald, what is it?" she asked, sounding mildly irritated. Then she immediately stood up. "Are you all right?"

"No," he answered. "Someone ... I think *something* is following me," he said between gasps.

His classmates stared back at him as his face flushed red. Tears began to stream down his face.

Mrs. Harper didn't waste a second. She crossed to him and took his hand, turning again to face her students.

"Please stay seated, everyone," she announced. Then she led Donald straight to the principal's office.

The school nurse was called in right away for an examination. She poked, tapped, and prodded. She took hold of his wrist, checked her watch, and made him stick out his tongue.

Minutes later, everyone seemed relieved that he hadn't been physically hurt, but following a brief, confused recounting of the events from Donald, who could still barely speak, the decision was made to phone the police as well as his mother.

It wasn't long before everyone arrived and the questions began.

"What exactly did you see?" said one officer.

"I don't know," replied Donald after a moment.

He was running his thumbs up and down a half-empty glass of water.

"It was a shape ... a dark shape," he continued. "It went behind a tree."

"Was it a man?" asked the principal.

"I ... I don't know. It might have been a man," he said with a nervous stutter. "I didn't get a good look. All I know is something was following me, and I started to run."

"Donny had a bad dream last night," said his mother with an uneasy, cautious grin. "He was convinced someone was trying to get into his room."

"Mom," said Donald. His face turned red again.

"It's okay, honey," she replied. Her voice was gentle and sympathetic. "I'm sorry, but I really think they should know about this."

"You believe he might have scared himself today as a result of having had this dream?" said one officer.

"No, I didn't," said Donald.

"It's possible," said the other officer. "A boy's mind can play tricks on him. Has your son ever been prone to nightmares before?"

"Not really," his mother answered. "He's a regular kid. A happy kid."

"This wasn't a nightmare, it was *real,*" said Donald, and he started to choke up again. "I swear. It was real."

"It's all right, honey," said Mrs. Gardner, and she squeezed his hand in support.

"We haven't had any unusual reports in the area," replied the first officer.

"But we'll definitely keep an eye on your neighborhood just to be sure," added the second.

"Right now I think Donald should go home and get some rest," said the nurse with a smile.

"Yes, thank you all very much," said his mother, and she stood. "You've been so understanding, really. Come on, Donny. I'll take you home now."

Donald felt alone and defeated as he rose to his feet and followed her out to the car.

No one would believe him.

And why should they? What was worse, his whole sixth-grade class had watched him wail like a little baby after he burst through the classroom door. He would never live that down, not in a million years.

Before she took him home, his mother drove past the spot where he left his backpack. He had forgotten to mention it to anyone at school during all the confusion.

The neighborhood was quiet and empty even now. It hadn't been all that long since his encounter with ....

Donald shut his eyes.

Mrs. Gardner pulled to the side of the road, and sure enough, it was right where he dropped it, not far from the large oak tree.

He stared at the area for a good long while, this time. Nothing looked bizarre or frightening or out-of-place. Just an ordinary shady yard with a nice tree in it.

He bent over to pick up the bag. Maybe his mind was playing tricks on him after all.

As he got back into the car, he noticed the zipper on his backpack was open. He rummaged through it for a second while his mother pulled away from the curb.

"I think someone's been in my bag," he announced. "Everything's been switched around."

She looked at him with a troubled expression.

"Is anything missing?" she asked.

"No," he said, checking again to make sure. "That's weird—it's all still here."

"I'm glad to hear that," she replied after a lengthy pause.

Her voice sounded odd to him. It was cheerful enough, but from the look in her eyes, Donald could tell she was concerned.

They arrived home soon enough, and he went up to his room and changed into his pajamas. Then he turned down the bed.

Not long after, his mother came in carrying a tray.

"I brought you some soup and a sandwich," she said with a smile, setting the tray down next to him. "You just need to rest now. Are you sure you'll be okay?"

He didn't answer. He couldn't look her in the eyes this time. He just nodded instead.

"I have to go back to work now," she continued. "We've got a big presentation going out today, or I'd stay with you."

"It's okay," he said. "I'll be all right."

"Jon and Chris are stopping by on their way home with your assignments."

"Great," he said, wincing.

"Try not to do too much," she added. "No TV or video games. Just sleep if you can."

He nodded again. "I will."

"All right. Call me on my cell if you need anything. I love you, Donny."

"Love you too, Mom."

A few minutes after she had left, despite the fact that he was still upset and confused, Donald drifted off into a much-needed sleep.

And he began to dream.

There were clouds. Thick, dark, and swirling.

Surrounding him.

Strange clouds like the ones in the sky over the grassy field outside his school. They grew larger now. Dark purples and grays. Soon the clouds were mixed with an eerie green glow that seeped through, penetrating around the edges. They were churning in the sky, changing shape and color, moving in and out of focus. In time, they became more crimson and red.

He began to grow weightless ... light as a feather.

A pleasant, floating feeling engulfed him. He was flying now. *Over* these strange clouds and *through* them.

Into them.

He could hear a deep, booming thunder in the distance. Rhythmic and steady. The sounds became stronger. Soon he could tell it wasn't thunder at all, it was the beating of drums. They pulsated in an uneasy, primal pattern. This was a celebration perhaps or maybe a ritual. The drums grew louder and increased in number, more ominous and threatening with each passing moment.

He began to hear strange voices chanting. Hundreds of them, maybe thousands.

At first, he couldn't make out their words. It was a phrase repeated over and over in an unfamiliar language. The voices grew closer to him, engulfing him.

Now he could hear the words ....

"*Ahn-tay ahk-mah gohl-inoo-ah vosh-koh. Ahn-tay ahk-mah gohl-inoo-ah vosh-koh.*"

Suddenly he heard a single unearthly voice that seemed to come from everywhere, echoing off of the clouds. Low and gravelly. Strained. Working hard to pronounce each word.

"Where do you keep it?" said the voice.

Donald didn't answer at first, then he began to shiver with cold.

"This does not belong to you," said the voice. *"Where do you keep it?"*

"I don't … know wh—what … you're talking about," replied Donald, finding it difficult to speak.

The clouds broke into fragments, and between his dangling feet, he caught several glimpses of the ground beneath him.

Donald was very high in the air. Tiny hills and trees moved by, scattered over a lush, green countryside. Strange-shaped domes gleamed and sparkled. Tall, gold-tipped spires jutted up from one or two of the isolated buildings, and there were small, ribbon-like rivers bending and twisting along their extraordinary paths. The water was shimmering like thousands of glistening diamonds reflected in the rays of a terrifying sun.

This was a place he'd never seen before, both beautiful and frightening all at the same time.

"Ahn-tay ahk-mah gohl-inoo-ah vosh-koh. Ahn-tay ahk-mah gohl-inoo-ah vosh-koh!"

He heard the voice again, in a low growl this time. It began to rise in pitch to a savage-like wail, filled with both longing and pain.

Donald was petrified.

"What do you want?" he shouted. "Who *are* you?"

"Tell me where this is!" hissed the voice. *"I … must … have … this."*

Donald heard a chiming sound, familiar to him.

With all that was strange and confusing, the one thing that made perfect sense to him was this chiming noise. He tried to focus his attention on it.

It was the front doorbell. He felt himself being pulled back into consciousness.

Donald sat up in bed.

His sheets were soaked with sweat, twisted, and thrown about. There was a breeze in the air, and he began to tremble from it.

A *breeze?*

No wonder he was cold. He looked around to find his bedroom window open with its soft shears gently billowing into the room.

His heart began to race as the doorbell rang again.

He glanced at his dresser. The drawers were each pulled out. Clothes were lying on the floor scattered in piles. His closet door was wide open as well. Boxes and games were removed with systematic thoroughness and set in stacks on the floor—their lids and tops pulled off and tossed aside. He saw his clock on the bedside table, too.

It was just past three thirty in the afternoon.

The doorbell rang a third time, followed by a loud knock. Through the open window, Donald could hear a familiar voice coming from the landing at the top of the cement steps outside. It immediately calmed him.

"Hey, Donny, are you in there?"

It was Chris, continuing with an irritable rant.

"*Can't* you leave your bike alone for one minute? Park it in the driveway like everybody else. Don't haul it up the stairs. We've seen it anyway."

"Are you asleep, Donny?" said Jon. "Let us in! We brought your homework," he added with a loud grunt, ignoring Chris's rude advice.

"Yeah, I'd be hiding from us, too, if I had *this* much work to do," said Chris, chuckling at the thought.

Donald jumped out of bed, leaned through the window, and called down to them.

"I'm here!" His voice was hoarse with an unexpected crack. "I was sleeping," he added, trying to catch his breath. "Something's happened."

"Well, in that case, let us in," said Jon.

Donald looked back in his room at the mess, and for the first time, he noticed an empty plate and bowl with just a few crumbs where his mother's sandwich and soup had been.

He hadn't touched any of it.

"I'll be down in a minute," he shouted. Then he froze. What if the intruder was still inside the house? He leaned out of the window again. "If I don't make it to the front door in the next thirty seconds, go call the police."

Jon and Chris glanced at each other, stunned.

"The police?" said Jon. "Seriously?"

"Yeah," said Donald.

"Do you wanna tell us why?" said Chris.

"You're not gonna believe me when I do," he replied. "I'm leaving now to let you in."

Then Donald paused, gathering every ounce of strength and courage he had before he ran through the violated home. "Okay, here I come!"

Moments later, the front door flew open.

Donald felt faint and out of breath but was never so glad to see his friends.

"What's the rush?" said Chris.

"That's *gotta* be a world's record," added Jon as he finished padlocking his bike to the railing. He turned to Donald and smiled. "Are you sure you don't wanna try out for track this year? We could use you."

"Come inside, quick!" he replied. "I need your help going through the house. Someone broke in while I was asleep."

Chris laughed. "Sure, Donny, that's a *good* one."

His friends entered and followed him up the stairs before slowing their pace near the top.

"Hey, you're *serious*, aren't you?" said Chris.

"Hold on," whispered Jon. "What exactly are we looking for?"

"You don't think there's someone still *in* here, do you?" asked Chris, getting upset.

"I don't know," said Donald as they arrived at his room. "Take a look at this."

"What the—" stammered Jon.

Their eyes pored over the chaos in silence.

Donald moved to his window and pulled it shut, making sure it was locked this time.

"I need to look around," he announced. Reaching into his closet, he grabbed a baseball bat and handed it to Jon. Then he took two golf clubs from a bag in the corner and passed the first to Chris while he clutched the second one in his fist. "And you guys are coming with me," he added.

Jon and Chris looked at each other. After a hesitation, they nodded in agreement.

With Donald leading the way, they searched every room in the house as he filled them in on the latest string of unimaginable events that began the night before.

Ten minutes later, they were back in his room, relieved that no one was in the house—but Jon and Chris seemed more confused than ever.

"Help me pick this up," said Donald, glancing around. His friends removed the scattered items from the floor as he continued in a logical tone. "Mom and Dad don't believe me already, so I'm not going to tell them about this. I'm just gonna put everything away."

"And pretend like it didn't happen?" said Jon.

"That's not what I mean," replied Donald. "But what's the point? I told them once, and they just think I'm having nightmares. So it's up to us now. We have to figure out what to do next ourselves."

"You really think someone's after your *shoe?*" said Chris with a frown as he handed Donald a T-shirt and one of his socks.

"Well, I don't think he broke in here just to eat *lunch,*" said Donald as he put the clothes back in his dresser. "Whoever it was, he didn't steal anything—and he didn't trash anybody's room except mine." Then he turned to them both. "He was looking for something. He must have seen me try it on after school yesterday. That's gotta be it. And now he wants to take it from me, so he's digging through my backpack and messing up my room to get it."

"But that doesn't explain everything," said Jon.

"Like how he got in and out of here during the day," added Chris. "Through your bedroom window, Donny—on the second floor, facing the *street.*"

"Or those weird clouds we saw over the field," said Jon.

"Or that dream I had this afternoon," said Donald in agreement. "While I was sleeping, that voice kept asking me where it was. I don't think I told him, though."

"The *shoe!*" shouted Jon with sudden realization.

"Where is it now?" asked Chris.

"Mom's closet!" replied Donald, but he was already halfway across the hallway.

Jon and Chris moved in right behind him as he entered his parents' bedroom, slid open his mother's closet door, and reached inside the tote bag.

He breathed a sigh of relief as he took out the silver shoe.

He was satisfied and even glad to see that it was safe and sound. Then he shoved it back into the bag and closed the door.

"Why don't you just give it to him?" said Chris. "It's not worth dying over."

"Yeah, Donny," said Jon.

"I don't think he wants to *kill* me for it," said Donald. "He could have done that a couple of times already if he felt like it—but he wants it bad enough to break into our house."

"*Twice,*" added Jon.

"And stalk you on your way to school," said Chris.

They were silent again while Donald ran through a list of highly unlikely possibilities in his head.

Things just didn't add up.

"Who could it be?" he asked them both after a moment.

But his question remained unanswered, lingering over their heads like a dark, ominous cloud.

Chapter Four

THAT SAME NIGHT at dinner, it was as if the afternoon break-in had never happened. The three boys covered up all traces of it long before Donald's parents arrived home. They weren't sure what their next move would be, but they agreed to meet the following morning at Donald's house. They would walk together as a threesome to school at their usual time. It was important that he wasn't left alone again to face his intruder, and Donald was happy knowing his two best friends believed in him and his story and they wanted to help.

"How are you feeling?" said his mother as he sat at the table.

Donald could tell from the glances going back and forth that his parents had been talking about him right before he entered the room.

"I'm better, thanks," he replied, trying not to get nervous at the thought of a possible speech coming.

Mrs. Gardner handed him a bowl of hot peas.

"Did the boys stop by with your homework?" she asked.

He nodded. "Yeah, they came by—and it's a lot, too, so I should probably go back to my room after I eat."

His father cleared his throat.

"I understand you had a pretty big scare today on the way to—"

"Everything's fine, Dad," he interrupted with a cheery tone. "I'm okay now. I slept all day, and Jon and Chris are going to walk with me to school tomorrow, just like always. You don't have to worry about it."

His father paused and folded his hands.

Donald could see that he was thinking—struggling with what he wanted to say next. Conversations like this never came easily to Bill Gardner. Donald and his father engaged in so few of them over the years.

His mother tried to explain it to him once when Donald was younger, not that it mattered much anymore.

Something about his upbringing.

Apparently Bill had been raised not to discuss personal issues in the home unless it was absolutely necessary, and even then it wasn't something to dwell on.

Donald had trouble understanding this—as much as he tried. The world had been a very different place when his parents were kids. His mom told him about the war overseas and the "politically charged era" here in the United States. She said Bill's mother and father had worked hard to maintain an idealized way of life— whatever *that* meant—despite everything that was going on around them. It was a survival tactic. And Bill was never allowed to speak his own mind as a child, which over time forged a wall of cheerful silence in the home.

A wall that would never come down.

Later in life, when he first met Donald's mother Ellie on a business trip, Bill told her she was "a breath of fresh air." She liked hearing it and reminded him of it often enough. Ellie said she was a headstrong young woman back then—comfortable with who she was—and Bill was crazy about her family back in Kansas. They were a little unconventional, but they expressed their emotions openly and opinions freely. He was drawn to them "like an oasis in the desert." That's how Ellie put it. Bill became aware of just how stifled he had been, growing up, and he was determined not to allow that to happen with his own son and wife.

Somehow, in spite of his father's best intentions, Donald couldn't help but realize that's exactly what had happened.

"All right, Donny," he answered with a resigned smile. "If you say everything's fine, I'm sure it is." Then Bill straightened up in his chair and hesitated before adding with quiet candor, "You know I'm always here if you want to talk."

Donald nodded. "Sure, Dad. It's all good, really."

"Oh, I almost forgot!" shouted Ellie as she checked her watch and bolted from the dinner table. "It's seven o'clock already," she announced. Then she rushed over to the television set in the next room and turned it on.

Donald and his father looked at each other with baffled expressions. They had a strict house rule about watching TV at dinnertime. It was forbidden, and no one was a more staunch supporter of this decree than Ellie.

"Mom?" said Donald. "What are you doing?"

"I just hope we haven't missed it yet," she muttered to herself. Then she turned and shouted again. "Bring your plates in here, guys! You won't believe this."

"What I really don't believe is that you've got the TV on in the middle of dinner," said Bill with a chuckle. "This must be important."

"Never mind your plates, just get in here. Hurry! I think this is it!"

Donald and his father obliged her by moving into the living room and sitting on the sofa.

"Donny, do you remember that stop we made on the way back from Kansas?" said Ellie. "That *shoe* I bought?"

An unexpected lump rose in his throat, and he nodded.

"What shoe?" asked Bill.

"I'll tell you all about it in a minute," she replied with a mischievous wink. "I've been keeping this a big surprise for you until it was on tonight. ... I took that shoe over to the convention center about three weeks ago and had it appraised on a TV show!"

Donald felt himself sinking lower into the couch. He could barely breathe.

"What shoe?" repeated Bill.

"Look!" she shouted with her finger pointed at the set. "See? ... There I am!"

George Clarke could hardly believe his weary eyes. Sitting in the middle of his one-room apartment in downtown Kansas City, he stared at the small, flickering screen perched on top of a cardboard mover's box. He put his plastic fork down on the bent TV tray along with a half-eaten can of cold baked beans, reached over, and cranked up the volume. Then he rubbed his graying, unshaven chin in utter amazement and continued to watch this anonymous lady with the long, reddish-brown hair, talking away about how she had paid a hundred and sixty dollars for a silver shoe offered for sale on the side of a road in Kansas.

When the camera panned down for a close-up of the item, George suddenly froze. Tears welled in his eyes. So many years of searching and hiding ... so much fear and pain ... had evaporated in a miraculous instant.

This was what he had been waiting for his entire life.

As he watched and listened, he stood up on impulse, reached his hand under the bed, and removed a rusty tackle box marked "Makeup" in faded black letters. He shoved it to one side, dug further under the bed, and pulled out a dust-covered shoebox. Popping the brittle rubber bands off of it, he lifted its lid with great care, then pushed back the musty tissue paper and took out his most cherished possession.

He held it close to his chest.

It was a second silver shoe, made for the right foot—the exact mate for the one he now saw through his tears on the screen.

The familiar appraiser fumbled with his explanation of how it might have been used, where it had come from, and its approximate age. George laughed out loud at how wrong this so-called "expert" was! It didn't surprise him, though.

The truth was too much for any of them—*far* beyond their grasp.

The woman smiled and nodded as the appraiser continued to ramble on about the unusual engravings. Again, completely off-track! They weren't decorative at all. The only thing he managed to get right was that this shoe was indeed made of silver with the most skilled craftsmanship this appraiser had ever seen, apparently. He didn't try to pinpoint its maker, since there appeared to be no identifiable silversmith's marks and no dents or flaws of any kind.

"Would you like to know how much my colleagues and I think it's worth?" he asked, which was a typical baiting question on programs like these.

"Yes, of course," said the woman. Her large blue eyes grew in anticipation of his response.

"We feel ... that because of its unique design alone ... along with the rarity of this level of artistry and the extraordinary condition ... at auction ... this shoe might bring anywhere from forty to seventy thousand dollars."

"Wow, really?" said the woman who was positively radiant now. "I paid a hundred and sixty for it! ... *Really?* ... Oh, wow."

George usually got a kick out of these price-tag punch lines, but this time, he froze in horror at the thoughts now entering his mind.

They would be coming for her, swiftly and directly, just as they had come for him after he'd found one of the shoes. That was over fifty years ago when he was just a boy. These people had their ways, though, and they would catch up to her soon enough. It had been far more difficult to locate *him* back in the early 1950s. There were no televised appraisal shows to broadcast his whereabouts, his face, and the shoe itself to a wide audience of viewers simultaneously. No super-sophisticated tracking devices or computer networks either. Those who had been dedicated to the confiscation of his shoe had to rely on eye witnesses and hearsay—and it had taken them almost two weeks to trace young George back to his family's farm in Missouri.

By that time, he already knew too much.

Then the pursuit began, spanning off and on for nearly thirty years, outlasting both his parents' lives, through many close calls, identity changes, and abrupt relocations, before he was finally able to shake them off, once and for all.

And George had been living undercover ever since.

A knot formed in his stomach as he pictured what lay in store for this poor woman if she tried, even just a little bit, to resist them as he had done.

But letting them gain possession of the shoe with all he knew about the impact it could have on the world was unthinkable.

Then his thoughts grew darker.

They would know what these shoes looked like now. Part of his success in hiding his own shoe had been that very few people had come in contact with it, so no one had given an accurate description of it. All of that had changed with this one broadcast. If they were smart enough, they would begin studying the footage ... replaying it ... *staring* at the etchings on its silvery surface. Analyzing them, questioning them. ... and ultimately trying to decipher them.

His thoughts grew even darker.

He doubted this woman's left foot was small enough to wear it, a notion that wouldn't occur to the average adult in the first place even if it did fit. He would take comfort in that, at least.

People were bad enough chasing after you, without ....

He shuddered as many long-buried, childhood memories came flooding back—those terrifying, unbelievable days that followed after he had innocently slipped the shoe on his right foot one lazy afternoon.

She could be in grave danger now.

He had to get to her before anyone ... or *anything* else did.

"You mean it's hanging in the closet now?" said Bill. "You haven't done anything with it?"

"Not yet," said Ellie with a laugh as she turned the TV off. "Why? What am I supposed to do with it?"

"I don't know. Put it in the bank vault. Or sell it," he replied.

"I don't want to sell it," she said. "I *collect* antique silver, remember? This is the highlight of my entire collection."

Donald was stunned as he tried in vain to recover from what he had just seen.

"I'm going to find a nice place for it here on the mantle, don't you think?" said Ellie as she moved toward the fireplace and stopped. "Right here next to my great-grandmother's silver key. That was her starter piece."

Bill shrugged. "Yeah, I guess so."

"What do you think, Donny? Did you ever dream it would turn out to be worth so much?"

"I ..." he said with a stammer. "I don't know. Yeah .... I mean I thought it was cool."

"Well, it sure makes up for those cruddy reproduction pieces I got stuck with," she remarked. Then Ellie sighed with a touch of regret. "I only wish my Great-Granny Sarah was around to see this. She would have gotten such a kick out of it."

That night, Donald decided to sleep with his baseball bat next to the bed. He wasn't taking any chances.

Before he turned the light off, he made sure his window was tightly shut and securely locked. It was only then that he noticed a small, dark-brown tuft of hair wedged into one of the corners of its frame. With a little coaxing, he was able to work it free.

He stared at it for a moment.

"Proof positive," he thought to himself as he folded it into a Kleenex and put it safely in his jacket pocket.

Thankfully the next morning came soon enough without incident.

"So nobody tried to get in again?" said Chris as they walked along their usual path to school.

"I doubt it," said Donald, swinging his bat idly back and forth. "I slept really hard, though. A *bomb* could've gone off, and I wouldn't have known it."

"Maybe we scared him away," said Jon.

"Yeah, maybe," said Donald. "At least I hope so. But before I went to bed ..."

He paused as he reached into his pocket and removed the Kleenex.

"... I found *this* stuck in the corner of my window."

Jon and Chris drew closer while Donald opened the tissue to show them the small tuft of hair.

"I can't believe I didn't see it there before," he added, shaking his head.

"Wow! Who cares? You've got *proof*, Donny!" said Chris.

"Yeah, I guess it's proof that somebody was there," he replied with a satisfied smile. He put it back into his pocket as they started up the hill again. "But nothing happened last night, so maybe he's giving up."

"I sure hope so," said Jon, frowning. "I really don't feel like cleaning up your room again."

Chris laughed. "Hey, I can't believe your mom was on TV last night with that *shoe*. Pretty crazy!"

"She didn't say anything to you about it first?" said Jon.

"She probably wanted to see how much it was worth before she told my dad," said Donald. "He's happy enough *now*, though. And this guy from the newspaper called this morning. They're taking her picture for tonight's paper."

"Amazing!" shouted Jon. "Your mom's a celebrity!"

Donald and his friends didn't notice the long shadow stretching across them as they passed by—the strange, dark shape perched on an adjacent rooftop next to a chimney.

No sound was made as it observed ... and calculated ... and waited.

Chapter Five

ELLIE GARDNER PHONED her office and told them she would be running a few minutes late. The local newspaper was sending over a photographer right away to take a picture of her holding the silver shoe, and she spent the next twenty-five minutes scrambling around the house, trying to make herself presentable enough for publication.

She had no idea that her fifteen minutes of regional fame would be considered newsworthy and figured it must be a "slow news day"—but, in fact, her phone had been ringing off the hook with enthusiastic friends and relatives ever since the broadcast.

Two of her co-workers even made her promise to bring it to work so everyone could have a good look. Reluctantly she agreed.

She was beginning to feel like a side-show oddity, however.

"Have you ever known me to keep a secret this long?" she asked as she removed the shoe from its bag and set it on her desk. "I mean, *ever* in your lives?"

"It's so *strange*," remarked Jen, who shared the office next to Ellie's. "I thought maybe it was my TV set, but that's really how it looks."

A small group of colleagues was gathering outside her door.

"I'm surprised you showed up today," said Ron, starting to laugh. "I figured you'd be sitting by a swimming pool someplace warm by now with one of those paper umbrella drinks."

"It's not like I won the lottery or anything," said Ellie. Then she rolled her eyes and laughed right along with him.

"Well, practically," said Barbara. "I know *I* wouldn't be here."

"Me either," added Ron.

Ellie grinned at them both. "Any excuse you can think of, right?"

"Hey, if I found a quarter on the street, I'd stop somewhere and have a beer," replied Barbara.

"If you had a quarter on you right now, I'd be charging you to see this shoe," said Ellie with a playful snort. "Hey, maybe that's what I should do—sell tickets!"

"After your story runs in the paper tonight, you might just be able to," said Jen. "What sort of questions did they ask?"

"Just your basic who-what-where-when-why-how stuff," said Ellie. "I'm sure I was all goofy with my responses, though." Then she looked down for a moment. "And what on *earth* possessed me to wear this blouse?"

"You look terrific as always," said Christine, smiling. "If I were going to have my picture in the paper, I'd want your wardrobe. Hey, do you mind if I hold it for a minute?"

"Help yourself," said Ellie with a welcoming gesture.

Christine took the shoe from Ellie's desk and brought it closer to her eyes.

"Do you know anything about these markings?" she asked.

"Not a clue," said Ellie, detecting a strange distance in Christine's voice. "But I'd love to do some research on them."

"Let me see it," yelled Barbara, who suddenly grabbed for it.

Christine pulled it away with an infuriated glare.

"Didn't your parents ever teach you two to share?" said Ellie in an attempt to joke with them—but the two women had very odd expressions on their faces just then.

Was she imagining this, or were they just trying to be funny?

Barbara's teeth were clenched tight in a ridiculous, forced grin. "I'd like to have a look myself, Christine, if you don't mind," she said.

Christine surrendered the shoe this time.

"Have you decided what to do with all that money?" asked Jen, trying to move on, but noticeably troubled by her co-workers' erratic behavior.

"Seventy thousand bucks is a lot," said Ellie with a sigh. "But I don't think I'm going to sell it."

"Oh, come on," said Ron. "That's some *serious* pay-off-your-mortgage dollars."

"Or travel-around-the-world money," added Jen.

"Donny would like that a lot," said Ellie. Then she grew quiet. "I just don't know right now. I can't think about anything except this giant pile of work on my desk. Now *go,* all of you, so we can get some stuff done around here."

Later that morning, when things had calmed down and Ellie had settled into her usual routine, the phone rang.

"I wonder if I might speak with a Mrs. Eleanor Gardner," said a soft-spoken man.

"This is Ellie Gardner," she replied in a pleasant manner.

"It's Mr. Owen Zeller here. ... I hope you won't think me forward by saying this, but I saw your delightful appearance on television last night, and I thought I might have a word with you about it."

"Okay ..." she faltered. "Do I know you?"

"I try to maintain a low profile personally and professionally. Let's just say I'm a great admirer of unusual artifacts, and your marvelous silver shoe has caught my eye."

For some reason just then, Ellie felt uneasy.

"Really?" she answered, and she began to tap her pen on her desk.

"Indeed," said the voice, almost purring with friendliness. "I was wondering if you might ever consider selling it. I would make it worth your while financially."

"Well ... I don't know," she said after a hesitation. "I collect antique silver, and it's the nicest piece I have."

"There can be no argument as to its appeal," said the voice.

"The appraisers valued it at forty to seventy thousand, you know," she quickly added.

"I wouldn't think of offering you less," replied the voice. "But what would you say to perhaps *twice* that amount?"

Ellie gasped. "You mean ... *a hundred and forty thousand?*"

"I do, indeed, Mrs. Gardner. You see, I'm a man who knows what he wants."

"Is this some sort of joke?"

"I assure you it's no joke," he said with a chuckle. "I was hoping I might meet with you downtown somewhere for lunch today to discuss my offer further."

"Well ... I don't know," she said. Then she stopped herself.

She felt uneasy again.

"Could I have a couple of days to think it over?" she asked. "Everything is happening so fast. Why don't you give me your number, and I'll—"

"That won't be possible, I'm afraid," he interrupted. "You see, I'm leaving for Europe tomorrow on a buying trip, and I won't be back in town for quite some time."

"Ah, that *is* a shame," she said, feeling a genuine sense of disappointment. Then she checked her watch. "All right, look—I could meet you at Jason's on Vermont Street at a quarter to one. How does that sound?"

"Not too crowded, is it? I don't manage well in large crowds."

"I'm with you there," she said in agreement. "It's out-of-the-way enough."

"Sounds perfect, then. And you'll bring the shoe with you?"

"It just so happens I have it with me at work," she answered, half embarrassed at the thought. "Some of my colleagues wanted to get a firsthand look."

"Can't say I blame them," he replied. Then he laughed. "Oh, but there's one more request I must make. If you don't mind, I'd rather you didn't discuss this with your colleagues prematurely. No sense in jinxing the deal, am I right?"

"Well ..."

"If you're happy with my offer, such as it is, and I'm satisfied with what I see today at lunch, then you can tell anyone you like about our arrangement. But I'm a superstitious man, and I wouldn't want either of us to get our hopes too high."

"I understand," she said. "All right. We'll have it your way."

A moment later, she hung up and began to tap her pen on the desk again.

Ellie was the first to admit she was lousy at keeping secrets. It took every last ounce of willpower to hide her recent television appearance from practically everyone she knew before it aired.

Still, this was different. She had only to wait until after lunch to spring the news on her friends at work.

But something felt wrong to her.

Why was this bizarre man in such a rush to buy it? As excited as she was at the prospect of coming out of their meeting a hundred and forty thousand dollars richer, she couldn't seem to shake this uneasy feeling over their conversation.

Finally her instincts won out, and she decided to call her husband at work.

"*A hundred and forty thousand?* Are you kidding?" he said with a cough.

"No, I'm not," she replied.

"You don't sound too excited about it, honey."

"It's just that he seemed so weird. That's the thing. ... It was creepy."

"So don't meet with him, then," said Bill, showing only halfhearted support of this suggestion.

"Really?" she said, a bit startled at the thought—but she could feel her tension lifting. "Yeah, I suppose I could just blow it off. But I'm sure he'd be angry, and that would be the end of that."

"So what? ... It's only money, right?"

"Yeah, but *lots* of it," said Ellie with a laugh. "Why does it have to be such a trap for us?"

"Okay ... so why don't you go ahead and meet with him for lunch—but don't bring the shoe with you. That way you can't do anything too impulsive, and you could see what this guy's all about—in a public restaurant, no less."

"But he's leaving for Europe tomorrow, and he—"

"Honey, come on. That's the oldest sales-pressure trick in the book. If he wants your shoe that much and he's offering you a hundred and forty thousand for it, you can bet he'll be back soon enough."

"I just don't like having it around," said Ellie out of the blue. "I get more nervous every second. There's something about this shoe, Bill. I can't explain it. It's like some sort of *magnet*. ... Everyone who sees it seems to want to get their hands on it—and it makes people a little crazy."

"All right, then. Why don't you swing by the bank before lunch and put it in our safety deposit box? It'll give you a chance to breathe for a while."

Ellie sighed. "I love you, honey. That's exactly what I'll do."

"Call me as soon as you're back. I wanna hear all about this meeting with Mr. Moneybags."

Ellie left the bank at half past twelve, relieved that she had taken a few extra minutes to put her celebrated shoe safely in the vault. She could feel the burden lifting from her shoulders as she drove toward her lunchtime appointment.

"Let's see what this crazy man really wants," she thought to herself.

Less than ten minutes later, she was walking along shady Vermont Street, next to the parking lot across the street from Jason's Restaurant. She liked this area of town. It was quiet, safe, and not too busy at lunchtime. She was lost in her own thoughts, waiting for a few cars to pass so she could cross the street, when all at once a gray van pulled up in front of her and stopped. A man with sunglasses and a dark, full-length coat got out from the front passenger seat. He turned away to slide the side door open.

"Mrs. Gardner?" he said with his back still to her.

Ellie was stunned as she glanced around, realizing she was alone on the curb.

The man turned again with a broad smile. She felt a strong hand pressing into her back. At the same time, a large white cloth was placed firmly over her nose and mouth from behind. Strong fumes filled her lungs, and she began to cough uncontrollably. Her thoughts went wild. The unthinkable was happening. She was being forced into the van. Her mind was spinning as she struggled in vain to cry out. Then everything went dark.

By four o'clock, Bill was getting nervous. He called his wife several times to find out what had happened, first on her cell, then he tried the office. Her co-workers seemed concerned that she hadn't come back after lunch, and no one knew anything about her plans to meet with a mysterious buyer.

He telephoned Jason's Restaurant next and asked if they had seen her there. The manager and staff didn't seem to think a woman matching her description had been among their lunchtime guests, but they couldn't be positive about it.

Bill also remembered the bank errand she had planned to run, and he decided to leave work right away to investigate. Sure enough, one of the tellers saw her earlier that day. Finally he was making progress! He took a quick look inside their safety deposit box. As expected, he found the silver shoe, but Ellie's visit would have been around half past twelve, they told him, and that was the last time anyone had seen her.

As the minutes slowly ticked by, Bill began to sink lower into hopelessness.

He arrived home just after five, and his son looked up from the TV set.

Donald seemed startled to see his father.

"You're home early," he said.

"Donny ..." began Bill with steady caution, "have you heard from your mother at all today?"

"No," he replied. "Why? Where is she?"

"Well ... I don't know."

Bill tried to stay calm. He sat next to Donald on the couch and took a slow, deep breath.

"Did she call you or say anything at all about where she might be going?"

"No. ... Dad, what's up? Where's Mom?"

"I can't be sure," he said, and his voice started to tremble. "But I think ... we should ... we should probably get the police involved now, so they can help us find her."

Chapter Six

ELLIE AWOKE TO find herself placed in a large, soft bed. Sunlight poured through the long beveled glass sections of an enormous lead-paned window just to the right. She was staring straight up at an impressive vaulted ceiling nearly thirty feet above her, with elaborate arches and an elegant crystal chandelier. It reminded her of an overly decorated medieval castle she'd visited years ago in the South of France. She had been abroad only once in her life. It was when she backpacked through Europe by herself, just before entering college.

Was she on *vacation* now?

Then, all at once, it hit her, and she remembered. She was a prisoner, brought here by force.

She raised her head from the pillow, and it throbbed with pain. Why would someone want to kidnap her? Where was she?

Her heart started beating faster.

"Good morning, Mrs. Gardner," said a nurse wearing a conservative white uniform as she sat reading in the far corner of the chamber. Her voice was pleasant, if a bit clipped. The nurse put her book down on an antique side table, then stood up and began moving closer to the bed. Ellie noticed she was wearing small, round, green-tinted glasses with gold wire frames. They struck her as odd for someone who was otherwise dressed so conventionally. "I trust you slept well," added the nurse with a smile.

"Where am I?" said Ellie, stammering a bit. "Where have you taken me?"

"I'm afraid I can't answer your questions just now," said the nurse. "I'm to see to your immediate well-being and ensure that your visit with us is as pleasant as possible."

"My *visit?*" Ellie repeated in disbelief as she began to gain strength. "This isn't exactly voluntary, you know."

"Good morning, Mrs. Gardner," said an unseen, familiar voice echoing in the room from several invisible speakers.

It was the man who had called her at work about the shoe. She struggled to remember his name.

"Mr. ... *Zeller?*" she asked after a moment. "What have you done with me?" There was a cold silence before Ellie felt compelled to continue. "Where am I?" she said. "What day is this?"

"It's been longer than you think," said the voice with a disturbing liveliness. "We've crossed several time zones since we last spoke."

Her eyes darted around the room, then paused with the uncomfortable recognition of a European electrical outlet on the floor next to her bed.

How could this be?

"Where have you taken me?" she asked. "What is it you want?"

"I thought you would have guessed by now," said the voice. "You see ... something was *missing* when we picked you up. You can't imagine our disappointment when we discovered it. Such a pity, too. This was to be so easy with no untidy complications. A simple course of action without incident."

"The *shoe?*" she replied, realizing what he meant. "Is *that* what this is about?"

"You must have forgotten to bring it with you, am I right? Careless of you, if I may be so bold."

"You would go this far to get it? Wouldn't it have been easier just to buy it from me?"

"I'm afraid we couldn't take any chances with our generous offer. *Far* too much is at stake here, and there isn't time for bargaining. Others will be following us soon, descending like ravenous vultures. Had you brought the shoe with you to our little meeting ... well, then ... we wouldn't be having this conversation at all now, would we?"

Ellie lay stunned in her bed. Was her silver shoe really worth that much?

"What are you going to do with me?" she asked. Her voice was shaking, and she tried to steady it.

"That all depends on how cooperative you are," he replied. "We need your help, you see. We want to know everything there is to know. You possess key information that we must obtain in order to protect our collective interests."

"Our *collective* interests?" she repeated, not understanding what this could mean.

"*Much* is at stake here, Mrs. Gardner. Your own life, for example."

She felt her heart pounding again.

"Mine, as well," Zeller continued. "In fact ... every living creature on earth could be affected by these next few days."

Donald and Bill waited helplessly while the police conducted their investigation. The local officers requested immediate assistance from the Kansas State Police after reviewing the appraisal show episode where Ellie had first divulged her story on television. They asked Donald and his father to pinpoint the location of the roadside convenience store, and they soon found the proprietor and his family. None of them knew anything about an unusual shoe made of silver, however, and they told the investigators they wouldn't typically notice if a dusty trailer had been parked outside or not.

The search for the mysterious woman who sold Mrs. Gardner her controversial treasure had led nowhere. Still, a composite sketch was created of the woman and circulated in the tri-state area.

It was during this initial round of questioning that Donald gave them the tuft of hair he had pulled from his window frame.

His father was stunned when he saw it.

"I don't know what to think at all anymore," said Bill, lowering his eyes and shaking his head. He seemed so lost.

"It's okay, Dad," said Donald with quiet reassurance. "I just hope it helps them find Mom."

The police were eager to receive the clue and sent it off to their lab right away for evaluation.

Then Donald told them about a second break-in that had occurred during the day, and how he and his two best friends hid the incident by straightening up his bedroom. As he talked, he found himself ashamed that he hadn't tried harder to make his parents understand what was going on at the time.

Bill listened in silence, detached and withdrawn, while Donald finished giving the police his official statement.

In truth, he was hoping his dad would say something—*anything*—even if he was angry or hurt or frustrated with him for pulling away. He needed his father now, perhaps more than ever.

Two days had passed since Ellie had first gone missing. The photo of her with the silver shoe ran in the local paper as a light human interest story—how her curious "roadside find" stumped a panel of on-air experts. The following day, that same photo was circulated to all national media outlets with an urgent alert. It was front-page news this time, along with the theory of her probable kidnapping and its connection to a popular appraisal show, as well as a mysterious, would-be buyer. Donald and Bill were assigned around-the-clock police protection after that. They were asked to turn down all interview requests, and their phone lines were tapped. They were also advised to remain inside the home indefinitely.

Several friends and neighbors began to show up on their doorstep in a comforting display of concern and sympathy. Some brought food while others offered words of inspiration and encouragement. The police weren't too happy with the constant activity, but Donald and his father insisted they be allowed to have people in the house. It helped them cope with the emotional strain.

At one point in the late afternoon, Donald was sitting on the couch with Chris and Jon, who had dropped by after school to check in on him. Three of their neighbors and one of Donald's aunts from Kansas were standing in the kitchen chatting with Bill when there was a knock at the front door.

A policeman named Finley went to answer it, and an official-looking man with a mustache and closely cropped, graying hair stood in the doorway. He flashed an ID badge and removed his sunglasses. Officer Finley nodded, stepped aside, and let him in. The man made his way to the center of the living room, then unbuttoned his suit jacket, cleared his throat, and began to speak in a loud, authoritative voice.

"Folks, I don't mean to alarm any of you. If I could have your attention for a moment ...."

Bill and his guests moved into the living room while the man continued in a calm, understanding tone.

"My name is Roger Powell, and I'm a special agent with the Federal Bureau of Investigation. We believe Mrs. Gardner's disappearance might be connected to a series of classified events. As a result, we will be taking over this investigation from the local authorities. I'm afraid I'm going to have to ask all of you to leave this house. Mr. Gardner, if you and your son would be good enough to come along with me, we'll need you now for some additional questioning. Officer Finley, I'd like you to remain on the premises and report any unusual activity. I apologize for my abrupt behavior—but as you can imagine, time is of the essence here, and I thank you in advance for your cooperation."

Bill looked stunned and turned to the policeman, but Finley gave him a confirming nod.

"We were tipped off earlier today that the FBI might be stepping in," said the officer. "I just didn't think it would be so soon."

As family, friends, and neighbors filed out of the house, Donald and his father grabbed their jackets and followed Agent Powell down the front steps to his car.

"Do you have any new information about my wife?" asked Bill as they pulled out of the driveway and started down the street.

"I've got a few questions for you first," said Powell. "They may seem strange, but your answers will help verify my theory, one way or the other."

"Sure, anything you want to know—but is she all right?" added Bill, and his voice started to shake. "I mean ... I just need to know. Is my wife still alive?"

Donald looked at his dad sitting beside him in the back seat. He had never seen his father this upset before.

"I have every reason to believe so," said Powell. "Where is the silver shoe now?"

"At the First National Bank," said Bill, "in our safety deposit box."

"Good," said Powell, checking his watch. "It's a quarter past five. We still have time before they close. We'll need to bring it with us."

"The police thought it might be safer to leave it in the bank. They said it could be the reason they kidnapped my wife. Is that what you think?"

"I'd like to ask the questions, Mr. Gardner, if you don't mind. We can't afford to waste time, and I need to find out several things right away to confirm my suspicions."

"Sure, okay," he replied with a nod.

"To the best of your knowledge, has anyone tried the shoe on?"

"Come again?" said Bill, thrown by the question.

"Has anyone put the shoe on their foot yet?" said Powell.

"I don't think so," he answered, a little hesitant.

"I did," said Donald, looking away. He was embarrassed by his confession, but he also understood it might help them find his mother. "I tried it on after school, about three days ago."

Powell was silent. Then he shook his head. "I was afraid of that."

Donald noticed for the first time that the agent looked tired and troubled.

"Donny, why would you do that?" said Bill. "Although, frankly, I don't understand what difference it would make."

"You saw the dark clouds after that, didn't you? And you had the dreams," Powell began.

"Yes," said Donald. "How ... how could you know?"

"You've heard the drums beating ... and the voices."

"Yes," he replied with a hush.

"And the chanting?"

Donald nodded.

"Have you mentioned any of this to the police?" said Powell.

"I told them someone followed me to school and broke into my room," said Donald. "Not about this other stuff, though. They never asked me about my dreams or anything. I didn't think it would matter much. ... Does it matter?"

"Good," said the agent, who seemed to relax a bit.

They were pulling into a parking space at the bank now.

"Why would my son's dreams have anything to do with my wife's disappearance?" said Bill.

"They have *plenty* to do with it if the kidnappers think she has these same answers," said Powell. "Let's get the shoe now. We need to keep moving."

Officer Finley phoned in his report from the Gardners' house that the FBI was on the scene. His sergeant wasn't happy with the news, however. He didn't feel it was necessary for one of his officers to remain on the premises with no one inside the home, but he took into consideration the recent number of alleged break-ins and decided to resist any bureaucratic objections for the time being.

Just when Finley had resigned himself to a solitary evening of sitcom reruns and leftover sandwiches in the Gardner home, he heard another knock at the front door. The officer answered it and was greeted by two men in dark jackets. Each of them flashed an FBI badge. Finley swallowed a bite of his sandwich, nodded, and let them in.

"I'm Agent Banning, and this is Agent Lamont," said one of them as they moved into the living room. "As you probably know, we're here to take over this case."

"If there's anything I can do to help you fellas out, just let me know," said Finley.

"We'd like to have a word with Mr. Gardner and his son, if you don't mind," answered Lamont.

Finley was amused by the FBI's apparent lack of internal communication.

"Ah—no, not at all," he replied with a smile. "But you're a little *late,* aren't you? They left with Agent Powell about thirty minutes ago."

"They *left,*" said Lamont, "with Agent Powell?"

The two FBI men looked at each other.

"You mean they're not here at all?" added Banning.

"They went with Powell a short while ago for further questioning," said the officer.

"I have a bad feeling about this," said Lamont to his partner.

"I'm calling in now," Banning announced. "Let's move!"

"Is anything wrong?" said Finley as he followed them downstairs and out onto the front porch.

"Plenty. For starters, we've been on this case for nearly three years now," said Lamont.

"*Three years?* I didn't know it was such a big case!" said the officer.

"Oh, it's huge, all right," said Banning as they reached the car. "We've been covering every inch of it during that time ... and we don't know anybody named Powell."

Chapter Seven

"WHERE ARE WE headed now?" said Bill.

He was sounding restless after Agent Powell had turned right, taking them onto a freeway entrance ramp.

"Just outside of town," Powell replied. "It's not far."

Donald sat beside his father in the back seat without saying a word for several minutes as he cradled the silver shoe in his lap. His head was numb from so many unanswered questions. He was tired and hungry and he missed his mother terribly.

"Did you ever wonder what those markings were, son?" asked the agent, breaking an uncomfortable silence.

"I've looked at them a few times," said Donald, thinking for a moment. "But I don't understand them."

"*Understand* them," repeated Powell. "Yes, you said it just right. They aren't decorations at all. How did you figure it out?"

"I don't know," said Donald. "I just knew."

"Look, I'm not sure what this is about," interrupted Bill, "but could you please just tell me what it has to do with my wife?"

"I'm going to tell you everything shortly, Mr. Gardner, because you both have to understand what we're up against," said Powell. "We're almost there. Only a couple of miles to go."

They were silent again until they exited the freeway and veered off onto an old dirt road that seemed to stretch out to nowhere. The sun was beginning to set, taking them deeper into a blue-gray twilight, and as they traveled further down the neglected road, they found themselves surrounded by tall trees. The road became more bumpy and uneven as the sky continued to grow darker.

Soon they were engulfed in the quiet shadows all around them.

"Here we are," said Powell.

He slowed the car and pulled it to the side of the road, stopping behind an old weather-beaten Toyota that was parked and left abandoned. There wasn't a soul in sight as he turned the headlights off.

In the immediate darkness, they could barely make out what was in front of them.

"Where exactly are we, Powell?" said Bill, growing impatient. "I can't say I appreciate this one bit."

Donald could tell his father was getting angry and maybe even a little scared.

The agent opened his door without a response, stepped out, and walked to the back of the Toyota. Then he reached into his pocket and found a second set of keys. After fumbling with them for a moment, he popped the car's trunk—and by the safety light inside, Donald could see he was searching for something.

Powell continued to rummage through its contents while Donald's father threw open his rear passenger door to get out as well.

"Come here, both of you," said Powell just then, as he gestured for them. He paused, wiping the sweat from his brow. "I want you to take a look at this."

Crickets were chirping with an alarming, pulsating rhythm in the cool night air as Donald followed his dad to the back of the red Toyota. Then Powell turned to them both, holding an old, beat-up shoebox. He removed its lid and set it down inside the trunk, next to a rusty tackle box marked "Makeup" in faded letters. Reaching his hand into the shoebox, he pushed the crumpled paper aside and took out a second silver shoe—a perfect mate for the one Donald now carried in his hand.

"Great," said Bill with a weary sigh. "So we have *two* shoes."

"Not just *two shoes*, Mr. Gardner, but a pair," said Powell, correcting him. "And these aren't just any old pair of shoes. No, my friends, not by a long shot. These *are* … the Silver Shoes."

"You say that like we're supposed to know what it means," said Bill, growing upset.

"Mr. Gardner ... Donald ... I'm afraid you've been deceived," replied the agent as he reached up with careful precision and began to peel off his fake mustache. "My name isn't Powell, it's George Clarke. I'm not an FBI agent. In fact, I've been trying to escape their watchful eye for decades now. I brought you here tonight at a considerable risk to myself as well as to you. But it's the only way I can help you find Mrs. Gardner and we can bring this whole ordeal to an end, once and for all."

"Now wait just a minute," said Bill. His voice filled with rage. "I don't know what you think you're doing here, but—"

"Look!" shouted Donald, staring down at his shoe. The markings were glowing with an eerie incandescent light as he held it out in front of him with both hands. "What's happening?" he shouted again. The light bloomed in intensity as it continued to seep through the shoe's elaborate surface from some impossible inner source. First, it was a fiery red, then a deep orange, then finally a blinding yellow blaze that flashed with sudden brilliance and illuminated the entire woods around them.

Mr. Clarke held his own shoe at arm's length with the same inexplicable radiance bursting from its markings.

They had to shield their eyes from the sheer force of it.

"These shoes haven't been this close together in over a hundred years," said George, trembling. "They're more powerful in this world than I ever imagined. We must work quickly now. Oh, yes, indeed. But first, I have to tell you everything I know about them."

"I wish you would," said Bill in a daze. "I don't understand what's happening."

All at once, they heard a rustling sound from the top branches of a nearby tree, and the three of them looked up.

"Quick, get in the car," said George as he moved to the driver's side of the red Toyota.

"What, *this* one?" said Bill, pulling up short.

"The Buick's a rental," he replied as he opened his own door. "We're leaving it here." Then he started to get in and paused to add, "I couldn't very well show up at your place as a convincing FBI agent driving *this*, could I? We're changing vehicles, gentlemen!"

The mysterious glow faded to a fiery orange as Mr. Clarke, Donald, and Bill piled into the dusty vehicle. George started its tired but reliable engine and made a swift U-turn on the bumpy road. They headed back toward the freeway again as George cleared his throat, took a long, deep breath ... and began his unbelievable story ....

"What I'm about to tell you will change the way you think about things—our world, other worlds ... and I only ask that you try to keep an open mind."

He looked at Bill, who stared at him from the front passenger seat, then he glanced in his rearview mirror at Donald and received the same blank expression.

He decided to forge ahead, nonetheless.

"When I was a boy, I found this shoe down by a stream on my family's farm in Missouri. I was barely ten years old at the time, out fishing on my own, when I spotted a shiny piece of metal sticking up from a mud bank near the water's edge. After I dug it loose and washed it off, I had my shoe. I thought it was the oddest thing I'd ever seen. No shoe had ever looked like that to me—and for some reason, I kept studying the lines and shapes carved all over it, trying to figure them out, to understand them better .... Before I knew what was happening, I'd put it on my right foot to see if it would fit. Then everything sort of *shifted* around me. Dark clouds came up and spread across the sky. The wind changed direction. Nothing was the same as it had been, and my foot was tingling with energy."

"That's what happened to me!" said Donald.

"Later that night, while I was awake in bed, I heard strange noises outside my window—like a wild animal with sharp claws or teeth. Something was trying to get in."

"Same here," said Donald as his excitement grew. "Did you tell your mom and dad about it?"

"Not right away," he said. "They would have just laughed and thought I was crazy."

"Yeah, I know what you mean," said Donald.

Bill turned and eyed his son in the back seat.

"I didn't think you were *crazy*, Donny, I thought you were having a nightmare. There's a difference."

"You didn't *believe* me, Dad," said Donald in immediate rebuttal. "Neither did Mom even though I told you both it was really happening."

Bill was unresponsive this time. He looked away and gazed out of his passenger window while George kept going, trying to overlook the obvious tension between them.

"At the crack of dawn the next morning, I was out pitching hay in our barn as part of my regular chores when I heard a loud noise in the rafters—like a pair of large wings or a huge canvas sail flapping in the wind. It scared me half to death. I went to the door and opened it wider, hoping I could see better, and I called up into the shadows. But there was no answer. Then came a voice like nothing I've heard before or since. As plain as day, it asked me what I'd done with it."

Donald gasped. "Who was it?"

"Even with the barn door open, I couldn't see a thing."

"What did you do?" said the boy.

"I ran straight to the house. Now, don't get me wrong, I was pretty brave back then—or maybe just ignorant—anyway when the sun came up a few hours later, I decided to set a trap for whoever it was, lurking in our barn, in case he returned and tried to scare me like that again. I figured he wanted the shoe all right, so I found an old piece of junk metal and shined it up good. Then I rigged a rope and hid it out of sight, just underneath the dirt in a circle. I placed my metal decoy in the center of it, and the next morning when I was out pitching hay again, sure enough, I heard the same voice in the rafters telling me it wasn't mine and I needed to give it back."

Donald nodded. "He said that to me, too!"

"So I gathered my courage and shouted for him to come down and take a look. I told him the shoe was sitting right there on the ground next to me, and I pointed to the decoy."

George suddenly stopped.

"What's the matter?" said Bill.

"It's hard for me to talk about this," he replied in admission. "Except for my parents, I've never told another living soul what happened that day. But it changed my life forever," he said, glancing at Donald in the rearview mirror with a look of warning. "It's about to change yours, too," he added. Then he took a deep breath. "Okay … I stepped out of the way and called up into the loft again, and that's when I saw it for the first time. It came swooping down and settled on the ground next to that piece of scrap metal, not more than a dozen feet from me."

"*What* did?" said Donald. He was shifting from side to side with anticipation in the back seat.

"It was an ape … a *monkey,* or so I thought … with dark matted fur and a pair of huge feathered wings like an eagle."

A stunned silence swept over them as Donald and his father let the answer sink in.

"No way," said Donald after a moment.

"Oh, yes, son—but it gets even crazier than that," said George. "This monkey looked down at that piece of metal, and I could see how angry it was getting. All at once, it started to growl. Then it glared at me with these dark piercing eyes and said, 'Why have you tried to deceive me?' It snatched up the decoy, which set off the trap, and I fell over backwards from the shock of it all. That monkey was pulled off its feet, high up into the air, and it swung there, hanging upside-down, flapping its wings like a giant bird."

"Hold on a minute," said Bill with a sharp tone, "I've seen and heard a lot of things in my life. I've even seen some crazy things *tonight*, but do you honestly expect me to sit here and—"

"*Dad*," interrupted Donald. "You wouldn't listen to me when I tried to say it before. You just walked away and thought you knew everything. I *believe* Mr. Clarke, because it happened to me, too."

"I don't think I—" began Bill, but Donald kept on going. His voice shook as he pounded the back of his father's car seat.

"We've *got* to listen to him if it'll help us find Mom! Please, Dad? Just keep an open mind for *once* and hear what he has to say!"

He looked down, visibly distraught, never having spoken to his father this way before.

"All right, Donny ... I'll try," said Bill in compliance. "For your sake ... and your mother's. I just need time. I ... It doesn't come easy to me."

Mr. Gardner fell silent as Donald recovered enough to continue.

"Mr. Clarke ... did anyone else hear the noises in the barn?"

"Not right away," said George, giving the boy a commendable look for his unexpected outburst. "My mother was working in the house, and my father was out in a field with his plow—but that monkey carried on, screeching like they do when they're trapped in cages at the zoo. After a few minutes, he began to wear himself out. His breathing was heavy, and he was exhausted from putting up a fight. Then he started talking again in plain English. He wanted to know why I'd set a trap and what I was going to do with him. He pleaded with me to let him go. I told him that all depended on how well he answered my questions."

"I can't believe I'm about to ask this ..." said Bill with subdued restraint. "Did he ever tell you why he wanted your shoe?"

"I got him quieted down enough that he gave into my demands. He told me things I never could have imagined," said George. Then he paused again and cleared his throat. "Now comes the hardest part. It'll be difficult to take in all at once. It was years before I understood what it meant for all of us."

Bill shrugged. "Okay, let's have it, then."

"Have either of you read *The Wizard of Oz?*" said George.

"Oh, no, not *that* again," said Donald, groaning. "A girl in my class teased me about it. She said our shoe was just like the ones in that book."

"Smart girl," said George. "She figured it out on her own."

"What do you mean?" asked Donald.

"Well ... what would you say if I told you the story was true?"

There was a deadening pause this time. Then Bill laughed as he struggled to find his words.

"You mean ... this was a flying monkey ... out of *The Wizard of Oz?*"

"Out of *Oz*—yes," said George, "ordered by the keeper of the Golden Cap to bring the lost Silver Shoe back from our world to its own."

"Back to the Land of Oz?" said Donald in disbelief.

George nodded. "And that Winged Monkey I trapped in our barn had no way of knowing about a man called L. Frank Baum, who wrote a children's book introducing the existence of Oz to our world in 1900. This creature, hanging there in front of me, hadn't the faintest idea he would be thought of as *fantasy*. But you see, that was the cleverness of Mr. Baum—his brilliant way of leaking classified information to the public. Frank Baum was forced to reveal the truth to save his own life and protect us all from a group of power-hungry men whose sole purpose was to rule both worlds. The details of Oz are all right there in his books for any of us to read, yet so few people realize it's *fact*, not fiction. He was working as an undercover agent for the United States government in the late 1800s. A highly specialized branch dedicated to supernatural events and paranormal activity."

"Sounds kinda like *The X-Files*," said Donald, growing more interested.

"*Not* your average TV show," said George in agreement. "This branch would soon become part of the Bureau of Investigation. A decade later, it became the FBI—but similar underground organizations have existed in one form or another for centuries now, primarily in Europe. In the 1890s, Baum traveled by train throughout the United States, posing as a door-to-door china salesman—a great cover for a secret agent, by the way—when he was handed the plum assignment of investigating the remarkable disappearance of a little girl named Dorothy from Kansas."

"I don't know how I'm supposed to believe any of this," said Bill. "This is a *children's* book."

"It took years for me to believe it myself," said George.

"Dorothy from *The Wizard of Oz* was a real person?" said Bill with a vacant stare.

"By the time Mr. Baum arrived at the Kansas farm, she'd already turned up again and was chattering away to anyone who would listen about a miraculous, untamed land ... where animals spoke and witches and wizards lived ... and magic was a part of everyday life. After hearing the details, he knew she had been to Oz."

"How would he know that?" asked Donald.

"Dorothy wasn't the first person to travel from our world to theirs, son—not by a long shot. For thousands of years, people have tried to find clues and information about one of the hidden portals connecting our worlds. Dozens have disappeared into them. Even one or two prominent citizens—but few have ever returned to describe the experience. Dorothy would be the first American ever documented who made the journey back again. This child was a wealth of information, too, and Baum knew it as soon as he began questioning her. So with a bit of financial compensation as incentive, he was able to persuade her aunt and uncle to let him conduct a series of classified interviews. He spent the next three weeks writing down every last detail the girl could remember, and when he finally filed his report with the agency, he mentioned she had come back to Kansas using a pair of powerful silver shoes taken from the feet of a dead witch. Dorothy explained that she had clicked her heels together three times, walked three steps forward, then everything started rushing by her—air, wind, and sky. She took only those three steps, and suddenly she was sitting on the grassy ground in Kansas again, sock-footed, in her own front yard. Somewhere along the way, those shoes went missing. Everyone at the agency assumed they fell off during the initial rush of velocity during transportation, but even with this accepted theory, an exhaustive search of the surrounding area was ordered. Nothing ever came of it. Still, there were those who refused to give up hope—and the case was never closed, in spite of the fact that nearly everyone associated with it believed those shoes were either lost, destroyed, or nonexistent in our world. ... But the three of us know differently now, don't we?"

"What happened to Dorothy after that?" said Donald.

"Hold on a minute—we're heading further out of town," said Bill as George steered the car onto the freeway again. "We're going in the wrong direction."

"Correct," said Mr. Clarke. "I'll tell you why in just a minute."

"We're crossing the state line, aren't we?" added Bill. "You're taking us into Kansas!"

"Correct again," said George. This time, he knew he had to come clean with them. "We're bringing the Silver Shoes back to the farm—or at least what's left of it."

"The *Gale* farm?" said Donald.

"That wasn't their real name," he replied. "Artistic liberties were taken to protect the innocent people involved. Their lives would have been ruined otherwise—which wasn't worth that sort of a risk. The family's surname was *McCollum*—Henry and Emily, like it says in the book. Not much remains out there now. The old house and barn are gone, but there's a small tool shed and rusty windmill that mark the spot where Dorothy once lived with her aunt and uncle."

"Look, I'm trying *really* hard to believe this," said Bill, reminding him.

"Why are we taking the shoes there?" said Donald.

George hesitated before he responded. He wasn't sure he should tell them everything just yet, and he was convinced he had pushed past the limits of what was digestible in a single day.

"Because it's a point of entry," he replied in the end. "One of the only places in this world where we know there is a portal leading to Oz. Dorothy's house was swept up into it in the middle of a tornado. She came back through the same portal. It's where the Wizard made his return trip as well."

"The *Wizard?*" said Bill with a laugh. "Next you'll be telling us *he* was real, too."

George looked Bill straight in the eyes, then responded with caution.

"Oh, he was real, Mr. Gardner. No mistaking that."

Donald leaned forward from the back seat as Mr. Clarke continued.

"And it's our misfortune to this day that he managed to come back in that hot air balloon virtually undetected."

"How do you mean?" said Bill.

"He returned to Kansas a few days before Dorothy did. His carnival balloon dropped down not ten miles from the McCollum farm, right into a large wooded area where he was discovered by a group of game hunters. He was unconscious at the time, tangled up in the branches of a tall tree. They cut him down and gave him food and water and warm blankets. They nursed him back from the brink of death. And as soon as he found the strength to speak, he started telling them all about this place called Oz, how he had lived in this incredible land for some time, and how, through a string of unbelievable circumstances, he'd ended up their supreme ruler—

the most powerful monarch known in their world. The hunters must have gotten a kick out of this ridiculous old man and his fanatical story—that is, until he reached into his pockets and pulled out a nice fat emerald for each of them. *That* got their attention fast enough. They probably didn't believe a word he said that day, but you see, the Wizard was highly persuasive. Before his time in Oz, he earned his living traveling all over the Midwest as a carnie hustler and third-rate magician. He knew how to get people to listen to him and how to hold their attention, too. So he started telling these eager game hunters that more riches than they could ever count were waiting for them in Oz, and if they could only help him find his way back, together, they would become the most powerful and wealthy men in existence."

"But how is this *our* misfortune today?" said Bill, who seemed genuinely intrigued now.

"The Wizard developed a loyal following among the game hunters and eventually their close friends—each of them wholly devoted to the cause. As their numbers increased, so did their passion and hunger for a better way of life. The Wizard's 'good word' spread to a chosen few, by invitation only of course, and just as he had done in Oz, this man orchestrated a master plan. He took control of the people's minds and lives, and an underground movement was born. They called themselves 'The Order of the Wizard.'"

Donald shivered. "Sounds creepy."

"Plenty creepy," said George. "It was a *cult,* is what it was. They worshipped this clever little man who would lead them all to 'the promised Land of Oz.' They would stop at nothing until they got there. So fanatical was this goal that they began to name their newborn children using the sacred letters O and Z to solidify their one true purpose."

"O. Z.," repeated Bill with abrupt understanding. "Owen Zeller."

"What's that, Mr. Gardner?" asked George.

"The man my wife went to visit the afternoon she was kidnapped," he said, and his voice started to tremble again. "He's the one who wanted to buy her shoe—Owen Zeller. We talked about it on the phone before she went to see him."

George nodded. "I suspected as much." Then he continued with renewed purpose. "We've got to get Mrs. Gardner back as soon as possible and take those shoes out of our world forever. They're far too powerful and dangerous here. Mr. Gardner, your wife's appearance on that TV show must have set off quite a chain reaction underground. I can only imagine the frantic activity going on right now. We have proof that both Silver Shoes are here in this world. Yours is for the left foot, mine for the right. What do you think would happen if they fell into the wrong hands now?"

"I ... I have no idea," said Bill, overwhelmed.

"By all accounts scientific and legendary, those shoes shouldn't exist anymore. They should have disappeared, dissolved, or at least lost all their powers before they got here—but they didn't."

"What happens if someone tries to use them in our world?" said Donald.

"No one knows for sure," said George. "Their combined force stretches beyond anything our imaginations will allow, particularly in a world like ours where magic isn't commonplace. Those shoes are older than our civilizations. They are older than the human race. Scores of higher and lower creatures of Oz have been destroyed trying to possess them. It's a matter of life and death for all who own them and all who seek to understand their power. That is why we have to act quickly now ... before it's too late for all of us."

Chapter Eight

SPECIAL AGENT STUART Banning and his partner Denny Lamont were certain this was another kidnapping, and they also knew what was at stake now. They had moved in a little too slowly after being caught off-guard when Banning took the historic call that a Silver Shoe had suddenly turned up on, of all obvious things, a television appraisal show. Despite the fact that decades had passed without a break in this case, the two agents had remained active on it for nearly three years, from the moment they first completed their training with the special branch. It was considered a rite of passage for all new members of the top-secret division. They were required to study comprehensive background logs and extensive chronological data and spent a fair amount of time searching for the whereabouts of a Mr. George Clarke—who, if he were even alive today, would be sixty-two years of age.

It had been thirty long years since the division discovered his last-known residence in a boarding house near Davenport, Iowa. They came close to capturing him that day, but his remarkable disappearance from the top floor of a four-story walkup was the stuff of legend, endlessly scrutinized and argued over by the experts.

For fifty-two exhaustive years, dear old George had been the sole possessor of what was now commonly referred to as the *Clarke* shoe, since it didn't take long for them to determine that the televised *Gardner* shoe had been crafted for the other foot.

Immediately a Code Red was issued throughout the division that after more than a century of theory and speculation, both of the Silver Shoes from Oz were verified to be in this world.

The ramifications, for all who dared to consider them, were terrifying.

As Banning phoned in his latest bombshell to their supervisor about a second kidnapping, the two agents headed straight for the First National Bank where the Gardner shoe was under lock and key in the vault. They arrived a few minutes after closing, but a quick flash of their badges opened doors again fast enough. The manager nodded with a nervous grin and confirmed that Mr. Gardner, his young son, and another man had come and gone a half-hour earlier.

He also mentioned they had opened a safety deposit box, but he didn't see them leaving with anything "unusual," as Agent Lamont so strangely put it. This didn't matter in the least. It was clear they retrieved the shoe and took it with them.

An all-points bulletin was issued within the hour to both local and state police, giving a full description of Donald, his father, and the unidentified kidnapper, along with details of a tan Buick they were last seen driving.

And it was during this time that the report came back from the lab on the tuft of hair that Donald had pulled from his bedroom window frame.

It was of an *unknown* species … most closely linked to primates.

The police shared this bizarre information with the FBI, who decided to have the evidence retested by their own lab, just for good measure.

Even at night, the Kansas countryside seemed familiar to Donald. They were driving through the northeastern section of the state with a surprising number of hills and trees and curving roads, not at all like the flat eternity that stretched across much of the region. As they wound their way past several farms silhouetted against a charcoal gray sky, Donald realized it was less than a month since he was last in this area with both of his parents.

Everything had changed since then. He remembered how he had longed for adventure during those final, precious days of summer.

This wasn't exactly what he had in mind.

A sudden wave of emotion washed over him as he closed his eyes and prayed for his mother's safe return.

"You wanted to know what happened to Dorothy, didn't you?" said George rather abruptly.

Donald looked up with a jolt, realizing he'd been seen crying through the rearview mirror. He moved out of George's sight, somewhat embarrassed.

"Yes," he answered, taking a moment to wipe the tears from his cheeks.

"I'll tell you what is known," said George with a diverting smile. "As you might have guessed, after Baum filed his report with the agency, they didn't waste one minute descending on the McCollum's farm like a pack of wild dogs—poking around and prodding—searching for signs of invisible portals or actual evidence of Oz. Poor Dorothy and her aunt and uncle felt like blue-ribbon science projects. Their place was ripped apart, examined, and catalogued for weeks on end until the family was pushed beyond their limits. Mr. Baum was pretty upset, too, since he'd gotten to know them well during his stay in Kansas. He felt responsible for what was going on, so he tried to convince the agency to leave them alone, once and for all. They wouldn't listen, though. Instead, they labeled him a troublemaker and removed him from the case. Frank was sent packing, all the way back to Chicago to be with his family and wait for any future assignments. Not long after, things took a turn for the worse. You see, by this point, the Wizard had recovered from his journey, and he'd gained a bit of a following. Nothing like the worldwide organization that it would become, but he had loyal friends with him now who told him about Dorothy's return just as soon as they got wind of it. They also mentioned the curious number of out-of-town visitors swarming around the place, so he decided to do a little investigating of his own—and he showed up unannounced on her front doorstep like a long-lost uncle. Dorothy was glad to see him again at first and gave him a great big hug, so they say. She started talking away in the parlor with renewed enthusiasm for all things Oz, now that she had this grown-up witness by her side who had been there with her. The Wizard listened with great interest as she explained to everyone about meeting him first in the Emerald City, the melting of the Wicked Witch of the West, and her eventual return to Kansas with the help of the Silver Shoes. I can just imagine he was a terrific audience for her, and the more attentive he was, the more Dorothy carried on about everything that had happened since her return. That's when the agents cut her off and began questioning the Wizard about his own experiences in Oz. But he refused to verify any of it. Instead, that conniving old rascal *asked* more questions than he answered, and he learned without much effort that the Silver Shoes had gone missing and our government was doing its best to recover them. He also learned about a portal or most likely *several* portals in this world, all leading to Oz. So, you see, in their eagerness to gain new information about the case, those agents made the fatal mistake of trusting him. The final nail in their coffin was when he stood right there in the middle of the room and denied ever having been to Oz. He laughed and joked and chalked it up to the charming imagination of a special little girl."

"How could he do that to her?" said Donald. "In front of all those people."

"That's the sort of trickster he was," said George. "After he finished, Dorothy burst into tears and started screaming at him. This was a total betrayal to her. She was so upset, her aunt and uncle took her to her room and put her to bed. The Wizard just shook his head with his counterfeit concern, tipped his hat to everyone, and quietly left the house. The agents didn't know what to make of him, but they didn't stop him from leaving either—in fact, they encouraged it. They backpedaled on the entire conversation and agreed it was a remarkable 'fairy tale' the child had told. But things just weren't adding up. There was no way this little girl could have known the details about Oz unless she had been there. So why would she lie about this odd little man being with her? They argued back and forth about it for several minutes until they realized how quiet it had gotten in the house. They decided to knock on Dorothy's door to check on her, but there was no response. They forced it open finally and found her room empty. Dorothy, her aunt, and uncle had disappeared."

Donald gasped. "Where did they go?"

"No one knows," said George, "but they vanished, according to the people who were there that day, never to be seen or heard from again—which is not an easy trick when you're under surveillance by a team of government experts. Believe me, I know from experience. And right away Baum, back in Chicago, was linked to their getaway as some sort of long-distance conspirator. When he was brought in for questioning, he refused to confirm or deny the accusations. Instead, he just nodded and said, 'What's done is done, now let them be.'"

"He was happy they got away," said Donald.

"I'm sure of it," replied George with a smile, "but that started an argument in the office. Baum told his supervisors that he detested the way they meddled with innocent people's lives while keeping such monumental revelations hidden from the public. Ultimately he resigned from the organization that same day, but this was far from over. The government refused to accept his resignation. It wasn't easy for a top agent to throw in the towel and walk away like that, and Baum was smart enough to know it, too. Ever since they'd ordered him back to Chicago, he was racking his brain trying to think of a way to remove himself from their division. It had to be an irreversible break, though. That's when he organized his notes from the Kansas assignment, documenting every last detail of Dorothy's time spent in Oz. He was determined to get the truth to the public somehow, even if it meant risking his own life in the process. There was a chance he might be doing just that, too—but he figured once the information was in print, their big secret would be out and the agency would stop this ongoing violation of private lives in the name of 'national progress.' They would leave *everyone,* including him, his family, and the McCollums, alone."

"But why would anybody want to keep Oz a secret?" said Donald.

"Greed," replied George without hesitation. "Oz is the pot of gold at the end of a rainbow. Think about it: an uncivilized land where precious metals and jewels are available in abundance but are worthless beyond their aesthetic beauty; a world where time stands still and aging is imperceptible; a place where animals can talk but could also be captured, harnessed, and trained to live as domestic servants or even high-functioning slaves; a place where magic cures most of the miseries of life—"

"But can also *cause* them," said Bill.

George nodded in agreement. "Oz may be enchanting and innocent from our point of view, but it's also a vast, untamed land and potentially very dangerous."

"Were we ever like that?" said Donald.

"If you go back far enough in history to the earliest days of man, there are writings, sculptures, and drawings that indicate we most definitely were," said George. Then his voice grew distant and reflective. "But that was a long, long time ago."

"What did Mr. Baum do after that?" asked Donald.

"Well, he realized if he published his report as written, it would be dismissed as the colorful rantings of a frustrated fiction author or even a bona fide *nutcase*. I mean, who would believe him? He had plenty of scientific evidence backing him up, but that didn't matter with something like this. Plus, there was a chance if people *should* accept his discovery as the truth, a national or even worldwide panic might result. He could never send it to the newspapers as is, for that reason alone. Then he got the idea to give it a *softer* twist—sugar it up a bit so people would take to it and perhaps even embrace it. This time, Baum constructed his entire report in the guise of a children's story. It was a struggle for him to do it, too—to make Oz digestible as a legitimate entertainment that would appeal to as wide and audience as possible in a short amount of time. He worked hard and fast, but in the end, to his great frustration, no turn-of-the-century publisher was much interested in what they perceived to be a modern American fairy tale. They didn't think it would sell books, and Baum was running out of time. He knew he had to act quickly before the government discovered his plan, so he decided to put up the money himself for the first printing. He risked everything he owned because he wanted it done precisely as intended, with no artistic or editorial changes, for obvious reasons. By the time his fellow agents caught on, it was too late. His children's book had become an instant hit with readers, and a second, even larger printing had shipped from the publisher before anyone could stop it. Soon *thousands* of copies were lining shelves of bookstores across the nation with a high demand for more. L. Frank Baum became a household name, and *The Wonderful Wizard of Oz* was well on its way to becoming a national treasure."

Donald smiled. "Did the government leave him alone after that?"

"Pretty much, yeah—although, at first, he received several anonymous letters warning him that if he ever mentioned Oz to the public again, there would be a permanent way to stop him from doing it."

"Death threats?" said Bill.

"A lot was at stake here," said George.

"What did Mr. Baum do about it?" said Donald in amazement.

George chuckled. "Well, he was a clever man, as I said before, and he didn't take lightly to it, that's for sure. He found a way to reach the Wizard by mail, which wasn't easy. That miserable 'humbug' went into hiding once he left the McCollum's front parlor that day. So Baum sent him a private letter. He also sent copies to his supervisors at the agency. And he warned all of them, in no uncertain terms, that if anything should happen to him or his family, he wouldn't hesitate to publish an explosive list, naming all names and revealing all restricted data about the existence of Oz. He knew people would sit up and notice this time, and it could blow the lid right off the conspiracy. He also mentioned that copies of the list were hidden in various locations around the country, and he assured them it would show up on editor's desks at all the major newspapers if he ever went missing or was harmed in any way. But even that wasn't enough for Frank Baum. He wanted to keep them nervous about it, so he set to work writing what would become a hit Broadway play based on his book, followed over the next two decades by thirteen additional Oz books and several silent movies he produced and directed himself with his own motion picture company. Audiences couldn't get enough of Oz even if they had no inkling of the truth, and Baum dedicated the rest of his life to keeping Oz in the public eye—although a few of his later stories came straight from his imagination, particularly after the sixth book. That's when he exhausted the remaining details from his original notes. He tried to *end* the series then, but by that point, the public was demanding more each year and he didn't dare disappoint. He was eager to ensure Oz's legacy, too. Instead, he dubbed himself the Royal Historian of Oz and continued writing right up until his death. So I guess he had the last word."

Donald laughed. "He sure did."

"Who would have thought?" said Bill in amused appreciation. "How did you learn about all of this, Mr. Clarke?"

"Early on, I was lucky enough to get my hands on a copy of the list—the one Baum was threatening to release to newspapers. It explains everything I just told you," said George, "and you'd be shocked by some of the people who turned up on it and the information he revealed."

"Thanks, but I've had plenty of surprises for one night," said Bill with a faint grin.

"I'm sure you have," said George, and he decided it was best to hold off on any additional revelations for the time being.

A moment later, they began to merge onto another freeway.

Donald yawned. "Mr. Clarke? How much further is it to Dorothy's house?"

"You're tired, aren't you?" said George. "And hungry—Mr. Gardner, you, too?"

"It's been a long day," replied Bill. "Do you think we could stop somewhere for food?"

"We're taking a detour into Kansas City now," said George. "It's only a couple of miles from here on the other side of the river. That's where I've been living for the past few years, in an apartment downtown. We'll go there first, eat something, then get some rest before we head out to the farm. We can't spare much time, though. And we have to be careful not to be seen by anyone. I'm sure they're out in full force searching for us now, and we still have to find Mrs. Gardner and bring her home safely."

"Mr. Clarke?" said Donald, growing quiet all of a sudden. "Where do you think they've taken her?"

"If my hunch is correct, she's far away right now," said George with a sigh. "About eighty years ago, the Order of the Wizard purchased a private castle, deep in a forest in Germany. It wasn't long after he passed away. The Wizard was a rich man by then, and it turns out he'd sewn hundreds of jewels into the lining of his coat before he made his departure from Oz. I guess he figured they would come in handy someday."

George laughed at his own observation before continuing.

"His wealth grew over the years and funded the cult. Today, they're a highly prosperous, secretive, and powerful organization with devoted members all over the world. You wouldn't know one to see one, so you've got to stay alert at all times. They live everywhere now, in big cities and small towns. Thankfully they're not hostile—or at least they haven't been so far. Their goal is to dominate the people of both worlds, not destroy them. Violence isn't on their immediate agenda unless someone gets in the way. They figure with enough financial means, knowledge, and power, they'll have little trouble in lording over the less fortunate. It's a dangerous philosophy, but sadly an accurate one. I believe they've taken your mother to their castle, hoping she'll bring them closer to Oz and to this goal."

"But she doesn't have the shoe," said Bill, "and she certainly doesn't know anything about its Oz connection."

"They'll figure that out soon enough, I imagine," said George. "They'll want to know where it is now and how they can get their hands on it—also, if she ever tried it on."

"What's the significance of trying it on?" asked Bill. "You sounded upset about that earlier."

"Because something *bad* happens," said George, eyeing Donald in the back seat. The boy avoided his glance, clearly afraid of what was coming next. "Since I speak from experience, I'll tell you what is known," George continued. "The best way to explain it is that all of the creatures in Oz ... the ones who've been searching for ages using every magical resource at their command ... can see exactly where the shoe is. Its power instantly transfers to the owner, but at the same time, it's like strapping on a tracking device. Believe me, it's not such a good thing."

"So, when I tried the shoe on the other day, that's when they knew where I was?" said Donald.

"I'm afraid so," he answered.

"And those clouds in the sky?" added Donald.

"A shift in the physical laws governing our world," he replied. "One of the portals opened up, and a flying monkey was sent through it by the keeper of the Golden Cap to retrieve the lost shoe."

"The Golden Cap," repeated Bill. "You mentioned that earlier. What exactly is that?"

"I wish at least *one* of you would have read the book," said George with a groan. "Whoever has the cap rules the Winged Monkeys. They are enslaved to it through a powerful spell. The owner is allowed three commands, then the cap becomes useless until it passes to a new owner. When Dorothy destroyed the Wicked Witch of the West, she took possession of it and ordered the flying monkeys to carry her back to Kansas. That was wishful thinking on her part, because they can't change worlds on their own. But when Donald tried his shoe on, a Winged Monkey was transported here just the same, with no means of getting home, except one. He was taught a simple phrase by his master—a series of words he could chant. They would bring him back to Oz as long as he had a Silver Shoe with him when he said them. Only the most powerful magician alive could have instigated a scheme as elaborate and coldhearted as that."

Donald thought for a moment, and then it dawned on him.

"Do you mean, *'Ahn-tay ahk-mah gohl-i—'"*

"Stop!" shouted George. *"Don't say another word!"*

He swerved the car, nearly driving it off the road. Donald and his father were tossed from side to side as the tires smoked and squealed on the asphalt.

After a moment, George regained control. His breathing was heavy.

"Whatever you do ... *don't* say those words again, son. It didn't occur to me you'd remember them. You're holding onto a Silver Shoe right now—and if you'd finished that spell, we might not have ever seen you again."

"I'm sorry," said Donald. He was out of breath himself and started to tremble. "I wasn't thinking. I ... I promise I ... won't do it again."

Chapter Nine

THE MARBLE FLOOR was cold under Ellie's feet as she folded her silk robe around her. She moved with steady caution toward the enormous window in the chamber, and through its beveled glass panes, she could barely make out the first crimson streaks of dawn coming up over the horizon. They seemed to reach out in hope from behind a row of snowcapped mountains that faced her medieval prison.

She was scared and confused ... and sad.

She had endured many hours of questions, most of which hadn't made sense to her. She didn't understand a thing about these people or their curiously isolated way of life—or the chanting she'd heard at sunset the day before. The frightening, indecipherable droning sounds drifted upward, echoing in the hallway just outside her bolted door. Hundreds of voices, perhaps thousands, raised in unison from deep inside the castle. It paralyzed her with fear as she began to grasp the scope of what was happening.

There were a handful of servants who had visited earlier in the evening as well, dressed in emerald-green robes with elaborate brocade. They served her dinner without speaking, then left minutes before the chanting began. Each of them wore the same remarkable green-tinted glasses like her nurse—and for some odd reason, everyone she'd come in contact with inside the castle had been wearing a pair.

She still couldn't appreciate the significance of her silver shoe, but she understood now that it was important to a great many people.

Through the ghostly intercom system, Mr. Zeller would talk to her and ask her questions. He had yet to show his face even once, but he wanted to know if she'd seen or heard unusual things—like dark cloud formations in the sky or strange animals crying out in the night ... or *inhuman* voices chanting in her dreams.

He already knew the details of a crime committed in her home, which unnerved her to the core. Ellie had been aware of Donald's nightmare, when he thought someone was trying to get into his bedroom, but she had no idea about a mysterious intruder entering the house the following day while she and Bill were at work and

Donald was asleep. Owen Zeller knew all about it, though—through her son's official testimony in the police report. Finally a frustrated Zeller asked if she even knew her own son's shoe size, and Ellie responded with defiant confidence. Then she heard several voices discussing something ... followed by a resolved, enduring silence. There were no more questions after that and no further contact from Zeller, either. She was left alone with an attending nurse to ponder what would happen next.

When Ellie first arrived and was coherent enough to walk, they had clothed her in fine silk pajamas and escorted her to bathe in a separate marble bathroom. Delicious gourmet meals were served on antique silver trays, although she hadn't found much of an appetite for them. But after Zeller's goading question in the late afternoon about the size of Donald's feet, the interest in her seemed to vanish.

It was clear she had been cast aside for more pressing issues. She assumed that her particular response and their obsession with the silver shoe were somehow connected. Did they actually think Donald had tried it on? Earlier in their interrogation, they asked *her* that same odd question, and they had listened very carefully to her answer.

As she gazed through the window, looking down over the tops of the trees in the valley below, the intercom suddenly clicked on.

"You're an early riser today, Mrs. Gardner," said an unfamiliar female voice with a soothing tone. "I hope you managed to get some sleep."

A nurse sitting in the far corner of the room jolted awake in her chair from the unexpected sounds. She glanced around and began to adjust her hat, sweater, and green glasses. Then she leaned over and picked up a toppled book from the floor.

"I suppose I did," Ellie replied with numb civility.

"Well, I have interesting news for you—but I'm not sure how much you'll enjoy hearing it," announced the voice, revealing just a hint of a sinister smile.

"Okay ..." said Ellie as she continued to gaze through the window, her mind filled with detached thoughts. She wondered just how far it would be to the ground below.

"It seems your husband and son have disappeared as well, and the infuriating part is we had nothing to do with it—can you imagine?"

There was a long pause.

"What's going on?" stammered Ellie as her mind snapped into focus again. Her eyes filled with tears as she fought to maintain her composure. "Won't somebody please tell me ... what is happening here?"

"I was hoping you'd answer that for *us*," said the voice.

Ellie gave in—and lowering her head, she began to cry.

"We're just as mystified as *you* are," the woman continued with faint irritation. "An unidentified man posing as an FBI agent drove off with your son and husband last night. They haven't been heard from since. The story's been all over the news. Oh, and I almost forgot—our sources say they stopped by your *bank* to pick up a certain trinket before we had a chance to do it ourselves."

"They have the shoe?" asked Ellie with fearful understanding.

"Yes, Mrs. Gardner, they have it with them now—and it's a shame, isn't it? ... Things are getting more complicated for you every minute."

Shortly after the breakfast dishes had been cleared, Ellie's nurse handed her a little white pill.

"Doctor's orders," she said with a cheery grin. "It'll help you rest."

"*What* doctor?" said Ellie, shaking her head. She pushed the nurse's hand aside with measured insistence, then continued to sit in her high-backed eighteenth-century chair, staring out of the large window.

"Now, now, think of it this way," tried the nurse again. She leaned in closer and rested a gentle but controlling hand on Ellie's shoulder. "You're not leaving this chamber for some time yet—if ever again, truth be told. So you might as well sleep, dearest. It'll do you no good to worry or put up a fight."

Ellie was shocked and looked up as the nurse continued.

"I'm sure you realize you're a long way from home now. This castle isn't accessible by outsiders who might sympathize with your situation. Actually, there isn't a soul around who isn't thrilled you're here, locked in this room. Better to sleep through it all, I'd say. Wouldn't you?"

"Why are you 'thrilled' I'm here?" said Ellie.

The nurse leaned in even closer, as if to reveal a secret.

"Because you've come in contact with a Silver Shoe!" she replied in a hushed tone as she beamed with excitement. "You've held in your hands the proof we've been searching for—the *key* to all that lies ahead for us."

Ellie lowered her eyes and nodded. "But I ... I don't understand any of this."

There was an awkward pause.

"No, dear, I expect not," said the nurse after a moment. She straightened up with a disappointed look on her face. "Perhaps you weren't meant to after all."

"Then what are you going to do with me?" said Ellie. "It seems I'm not much use to you anymore."

The nurse stared at her with a vacant expression, peering down from behind her round, green-tinted glasses. Her empty eyes sent an unexpected chill through Ellie.

"That is not for me to say," she answered.

Then she held the pill out again in the palm of her hand.

This time, Ellie accepted it.

"Believe me, it's for the best," added the nurse, turning away. "Let me get you some water," she said as she crossed the room to a nightstand by the large bed.

On impulse, Ellie shoved the pill under an embroidered placemat in front of her before the nurse turned again, holding a crystal water glass.

Ellie pretended to take the pill with the water, gulping several times from the glass.

"There now, isn't that better?" asked the nurse.

"I suppose it is. Thank you, Mrs.—"

"It's Zavian, dear," she interrupted. "Olive Zavian. But you can call me Olive if you like. No sense in formalities here."

"Thank you, Olive. I'm curious—why does everyone wear those green glasses?"

"Our eyes need time to adjust," she replied with a blissful smile. "No human being can look directly at the splendor that awaits us. We must be prepared for it when the time comes."

Ellie nodded. "I see." She was grateful for the explanation but had no idea what it meant. "I should lie down now," she added.

"Of course, dear."

The nurse helped her to the bed. Then Ellie climbed in, pulling the covers up around her.

"Would you care for some tea before your nap?" said Olive.

"No ... thank you. But please help yourself."

"Don't mind if I do," said Olive with a giggle.

There was something equally charming and disturbing about this woman. Ellie didn't dare trust her. She figured the nurse's loyalties were with the group—yet she had shown compassion, in a strange way.

Ellie watched her lift the pot from the table as a loud metal clank came from just outside the thick, wooden door.

Someone was unlocking it.

A man opened it wide and stepped into the room.

"Zeller is on the phone. He wants to speak with you at once," the man announced.

"Certainly," Olive replied.

She set the teapot down, crossed to the door, then turned toward Ellie.

"Mrs. Gardner is going to sleep now," said Olive to the man. "Bolt the door behind us. Everything should be fine while I'm away. I won't be long."

"Very good," he said.

The two of them left together. Then moments later, Ellie heard a loud clank again, signaling she was trapped inside the chamber.

This time, she was alone—and in the split second of silence that followed, the initial stages of a plan came to her.

She had no idea whether it would work or not—or what to expect even if it did. It was a million-to-one shot, but she had to risk it.

She got out of bed and went over to the breakfast table. She lifted a corner of the placemat and found the sleeping pill underneath it. She removed the lid from the teapot and dropped the pill inside. Grabbing a silver spoon next to the pot, she stirred it a few times.

Then Ellie got back into bed and pretended to be asleep.

She had only to wait now ... and hope that when her nurse returned, she still wanted to have some tea.

"Wow, this is where you live?" said Donald, stunned by the small studio apartment.

"I'll bet you were expecting the Ritz Hotel," said George with a sheepish smile. He set the overstuffed McDonald's bags down on the bent TV tray. "Considering the life I've led, I'd say this would be expected. You two can take the bed. I'll be fine on the floor."

Donald and his father looked around the sparse room.

There was a queen-sized mattress on a plain iron frame in one corner. A single threadbare armchair faced an old nineteen-inch TV set that was perched on top of a cardboard mover's box. The walls were dingy white with nothing on them, the carpet was a typical brown, but the room was clean enough. Donald thought it looked barely occupied, though.

"How long have you lived here?" said Bill.

"About nine years now," replied George, reaching across to turn on the TV. Then he opened the first bag of food. "Donny, here's your burger," he added, holding out a wrapped sandwich. "Fries are in the other bag. ... Mr. Gardner?"

"Call me Bill," he said with a somewhat awkward but agreeable smile. "It must have been hard for you," he went on as he took the burger from George. "All those years living in seclusion, never knowing when you might have to move again."

"Yeah ..." said George with a nod. "Well, it's been interesting, that's for sure."

"Why did you do it?" said Bill. "I mean, why didn't you just give the agents the shoe when they first came looking for it? Wouldn't that have been easier?"

"Easier?" repeated George as he pondered the question. "I don't know, Bill." He took another moment to consider it. "I'm not sure if my life would have been easier knowing I handed our government the single most powerful weapon they'll likely ever get their hands on."

After swallowing a bite, Bill continued. "You said yourself that one shoe alone wouldn't be capable of much."

"*Probably* wouldn't," said George.

"You were just a kid back then, but you gave up the rest of your freedom for—"

"For the satisfaction of knowing I might help others keep theirs," finished George. "Don't make me out to be such a hero. Countless people have done the same thing. Besides, I *was* a scared little kid, as you said—and I could see what those men were up to. I didn't want to be locked away and tortured and tested like—"

He stopped himself.

"Like what?" said Bill.

"Hey, look!" shouted Donald. "Turn up the sound! We're on TV!"

George cranked the volume as an anchorman continued with his top story.

"Can you beat that?" said George moments later. "We're headline news!"

"It isn't every day a whole family is systematically kidnapped," said Bill with a chuckle. He sounded oddly removed from the crime unfolding in front of his eyes, yet he was watching pictures of himself, his wife, and Donald ... their home ... interviews with his friends and neighbors .... Then he turned away from it, growing restless. "People will be worried about us. I should make a couple of calls."

"You realize you can't," said George. "It could jeopardize everything. I know it's hard, but you must understand this is the only way."

"I hate that picture of me," said Donald with a loud grunt. "Why did they have to show *that* one? I'll bet Aunt Jenny gave it to them."

"At least they haven't figured out who *you* are yet," said Bill, glancing at George.

"No, they haven't," he replied, "and we've got to keep it that way as long as possible. As soon as they discover I'm still alive—that I'm the 'unidentified man' who drove off with you—they'll know we have both shoes with us. I can only imagine the armies that would come looking for us then."

"What are we going to do about it?" asked Bill.

"Catch some sleep, then hit the road again," said George. "We've got to get to the McCollum farm as soon as possible. After that ... I just hope we find what we're looking for."

"What's that?" asked Donald.

"The last bit of information that will help us bring your mother home again and take these shoes out of our world forever."

Although Donald's mind was racing with everything he'd learned that day, exhaustion won over, and he fell into a deep sleep as soon as his head hit the pillow. It was shortly after midnight when they turned out the lights.

Banning slowed the car. They could see the back of a tan Buick in their headlights now.

Beyond that, they saw the strobing red flashes of a police vehicle parked beside the dirt road. An officer stood next to it with a middle-aged man in jeans and a Kansas City Royals baseball cap. The officer stepped into the road and waved them down.

"Officer, I'm Agent Banning—this is Agent Lamont," he said moments later as he approached the two men and extended his hand for a shake. "Thank you for staying up so late to talk with us."

"It looks like this could be the car, all right," said Lamont, scanning his flashlight over the abandoned Buick.

Banning's stomach tightened at the prospect of losing the Gardners and their kidnapper yet again.

"I'm Officer Wilson. This here is Mr. Samuel Atkinson," said the policeman, shaking the agent's hand. "He's the gentleman who phoned us about the bright light."

"Mr. Atkinson, we'd appreciate any information you can give us," said Banning. "It's an important case."

"Well, I didn't see much," replied Sam as he lifted his cap and scratched the top of his head. "I was out walkin' about a hundred yards or so from this spot when I saw a bright light ahead of me. It was nearly dark, and it was kinda hard to make out the details, you know? Looked like it was comin' from the side of the road, right about here," he added. "I never seen anything like it before in my life. Sorta shook me up."

"What kind of a light?" asked Lamont.

"Huge!" said Sam with a chuckle. "It started out all red and orange. Then it just kept getting brighter. Lit up this whole area like sunlight. I could see the trees in front of me, plain as day."

"What happened next?" said Banning, growing excited.

"Well, I stopped dead in my tracks and just stared at it," said Sam. "Then I got to wonderin' if somebody might be hurt, you know? So I started runnin' up the road. The light was fading again, but I could still see these three people standing next to an old car right here." He pointed to the space in front of the abandoned Buick. "I gotta tell ya, I didn't get much of a look at 'em. By the time I was close enough, they were already in the car. Then they turned around and drove off quick, headin' back toward the freeway."

"Did you get a good look at the car?" asked Lamont.

"It's hard say—even with the bright light," replied Sam, hesitating. "But I think it was a Toyota, most likely. Near as I could tell. Maybe fifteen years old or so. Like they used to make 'em. *Red*, I think. ... Funny thing, though. They left this brand new Buick sittin' here by the road, keys and all!"

Olive returned from her phone conversation with Zeller a few minutes later and was walking around inside the chamber.

Ellie could hear each step she took on the marble floor, but she didn't dare twitch a muscle. She lay motionless, her breathing regular, her eyes closed, while she prayed for a miracle. After what seemed like an endless silence, she heard the soft tinkle of a silver spoon tapping against the edge of a china cup. She strained her ears to make it wasn't her imagination.

Sure enough, Olive had remembered about the tea.

Ellie relaxed, but forced herself to remain awake and alert. Although she was exhausted, it would ruin everything if she actually *slept* through her one chance to escape.

She waited in endless limbo as thoughts of Bill and Donald entered her mind. She tried not to grow distracted. She had to stay focused.

Ellie trusted they were all right. Allowing herself to believe otherwise, even for an instant, would be too much for her.

The minutes passed—perhaps even hours.

She had no idea how much time it was before she heard another noise.

Something had fallen to the floor.

Ellie counted to ten, then rolled over and stole a quick peek across the room. She spotted Olive right away in her usual chair.

Success!

With great care, she sat up to make sure it was true. The nurse had dropped her book to the floor again and was leaning back, slouched in the chair, unconscious.

Ellie's heart started to race.

She would try to leave the castle now and go for help, determined to make this work.

She got out of bed and crossed to the window. Reaching behind the velvet drapes to the right, she located an iron crank. She had seen a servant using it earlier. It seemed to be the only way to adjust these enormous glass panes.

She rotated the archaic device, hoping it wouldn't be too loud. Even with Olive out cold from a dose of her own medicine, Ellie wasn't about to risk waking her.

After a minute, the large panel next to her had swung out far enough, allowing her to lean over and have a look.

She felt an icy breeze against her skin right away, which revived her. She was more alert now and more scared than ever.

As she cast her eyes downward, she discovered just how high up she was—over two hundred feet to the steep hillside below, she estimated.

Then she noticed a narrow balcony extending from the tower wall, with a solid iron railing around it. It was just to the left of her window, about thirty feet beneath her.

She swallowed hard, trying not to think about the danger involved in attempting to reach it. Ellie had seen plenty of old movies where prisoners escaped by tying bed linens together and lowered themselves out of windows or over walls. The idea seemed ludicrous at the time, but it was the best she could come up with for now.

Without hesitation, she went back to her bed and pulled the oversized sheets off.

It felt like a dream. The notion of creating a makeshift rope and shimmying down the side of a castle tower was utterly surreal. Nevertheless, she joined two ends of the thick satin sheets in her hands and formed a tight knot. She gave each end a good strong tug for safety ... and watched them pull apart with little resistance.

She tried once more, using the only other knot she'd ever learned as a Girl Scout, but they still separated.

Ellie hurled the slippery sheets to the floor in frustration and clutched herself. She was sick to her stomach with fear.

Then she rose to her feet with fists clenched and circled the chamber a few times, trying hard to think of what to do next.

She glanced at Olive again, sitting in her chair ...

... when another idea occurred to her.

She would have to work fast, though. The gilded clock in the far bookcase told her it was nearly lunchtime. The servants would be arriving soon with her food.

Ellie crossed to the sleeping nurse and nudged her, but Olive didn't wake up.

This plan might work, she thought.

With great care, she removed Olive's green-tinted glasses and nurse's cap, along with a few hairpins, and set them down on the table beside her. Then she reached across and began to undo the buttons on Olive's white wool cardigan, next came the nurse's uniform ....

Ellie proceeded to undress herself after that, and in less than eight minutes, she had managed to switch clothes completely with the unconscious nurse.

She reached under Olive's arms, lifted her up, and dragged her to the bed. Ellie made sure Olive was lying on her side with her face turned away from the door and the sheets pulled up around her.

Then, all at once, she heard a familiar clank outside her room.

Ellie ran across the chamber, sat in Olive's chair, and took a deep breath. At the last possible second, she leaned forward, grabbed the book from the floor, and pretended to read from it ... as the thick wooden door opened wide.

Two servants entered, dressed in the same elaborate green robes from the previous night. They were carrying trays of food.

"Don't bother to wake her," said Ellie with casual inflection, trying to sound as much like Olive as possible. "I gave her a pill about an hour ago. Zeller wants her to sleep."

"What about all this food?" said one of the drones. He didn't look up. "Should we leave it here or come back later?"

"Leave the meal, please," said Ellie with an appreciative smile. Then she peered over the top of Olive's book through her green-tinted glasses. The drones seemed much too occupied arranging the table to be suspicious of any wrongdoing.

Ellie's plan was actually working!

She glanced back at the book and was startled to discover that it was a plainly-bound, early edition of *The Wonderful Wizard of Oz* by L. Frank Baum.

"I'm certain Mrs. Gardner will eat something when she wakes," Ellie continued, trying to focus on her mission again. "Oh—and if you wouldn't mind staying a moment—it seems I left my watch downstairs when I spoke with Zeller this morning. I'd like to run and get it."

Her heart pounded as she set the book on the edge of the table and stood up.

"We don't mind," said the other drone. "But hurry back, or we'll be late for Program."

Ellie hesitated at the entrance, facing away from them.

"Of course," she replied. "I won't be but a minute."

Then she closed the heavy door behind her ... and locked it.

She was free.

Ellie had never been more than a few feet outside the chamber—and she was unfamiliar with this castle. She knew that the small passageway in front of her led to the marble bathroom on the left, so she decided to go to the right this time and found herself moving through an immense corridor. She passed several torches burning brightly, despite the midday hour. They were bolted to the walls at regular intervals and gave off warmth and faint pools of flickering green light that reflected onto the high arches above her. Further ahead, she came across a dozen narrow windows in the Brick Gothic style, overlooking a meticulously manicured courtyard. She also noticed the expansive valley and forest stretching beyond it as she hurried along.

Ellie tried to calm herself, realizing it was true—this castle was entirely isolated in the wilderness.

She knew she couldn't appear to be in a rush, in case she encountered suspicious eyes along the way.

Ellie reached the end of the long corridor and stopped short in front of a painting on the wall opposite her. It was overwhelming.

An enormous eighteenth-century landscape—a beautiful vista of an extravagant, ornate city gleaming on the horizon, as seen from the edge of a lovely country meadow. The detailed architecture seemed odd to her, and so did the colors. Then she remembered Olive's green glasses and removed them from her face. The sky was utterly fantastic, like nothing she'd ever experienced, and the buildings each had twinkling accents sparkling like jewels, almost like dazzling emeralds ....

"If I didn't know better, I'd say this was the Emerald City," she thought to herself with a puzzled frown. She was certain her abnormal deduction had something to do with Olive's surprising choice of literature.

There was a small, unrecognizable signature in the bottom right-hand corner of the painting, with the date of 1794 underneath it.

Ellie stared at the round, green-tinted glasses in her hands before putting them on again slowly. Then she dismissed her ridiculous notion and turned to the left, spotting a spiral staircase at the end of a short hallway.

It occurred to her that the castle was empty, not a soul around.

Where *was* everybody? Attending another mass gathering, no doubt.

No time to worry about it.

She began to descend the narrow stairs ... when suddenly it started again—the legions of voices chanting with escalating fervor in a language she didn't recognize. Their booming, rhythmic sounds drifted upward through the dark stairwell. She wanted to turn and run, but there was no time for backtracking. She needed to find the quickest way out of the castle before she was discovered.

As she stood frozen at the top of the ancient stone steps, trying to decide which way to go, curiosity began to get the best of her.

She *had* to find out what they were doing ... and saying ... and what it all meant.

Ellie held her breath, said a silent prayer, then continued slowly down the narrow stairs toward the voices.

Chapter Ten

THERE WERE THICK clouds swirling. Murky and intense. Deep shadowy purples with a green glow around the edges, just like before. But Donald wasn't floating in them this time. He was walking at a steady pace through a densely wooded area nestled against a steep hill.

As the eerie haze lifted, the light faded along with it until he could scarcely see what was in front of him.

He ducked under the heavy branches that barred his way. His heart pounded, but he kept on going, zigzagging as he moved in order to avoid colliding with one of the immense trunks. Now and then, a fallen twig cracked under his feet, startling him with the uncomfortable announcement of his presence in the woods.

Where was he?

He spotted a shimmering mist ahead. It flickered with enticement through the labyrinth of trees as it gave off a faint gray glow, devoid of all warmth. A *hopeless* color, in fact. Draining and debilitating.

Yet out of some hypnotic compulsion, he was drawn to it.

He moved closer and began to hear water splashing just a few yards from where he stood. It was a shallow creek winding its way through the forest. Looking up, he saw the stars scattered across the sky, fighting to make themselves known through a web of twisted upper branches.

Donald was drowning in the sheer density of these unfamiliar woods. He lowered his gaze again and concentrated on the mist in front of him as a sickening feeling swept over him—and he began to understand *exactly* what was up ahead ....

He sat up in bed.

He had to think for a moment. The digital clock next to him said 4:33 AM in glowing red numbers. It was dark in George's studio apartment except for a single bug light outside the front door that cast an odd yellow sheen over the second-floor walkway. It penetrated in tiny horizontal shafts through the metal blinds of the window next to it.

Something had woken him up.

Donald looked around and squinted, trying to adjust his eyes. He could hardly see his father sleeping next to him. Mr. Clarke was slumbering on the floor, curled up with a blanket and pillow. Donald spotted his silhouette, and it reassured him.

All of a sudden, he heard a scratching noise coming from the window. His heart pounded with recognition as he watched a familiar shadow pass in front of the blinds, eclipsing the light.

He reached across the bed and shook his father awake.

"Dad!" he whispered. "Dad, wake up!"

Mr. Gardner rolled over and rubbed his eyes.

"What is it, Donny?" he asked in a sluggish daze. "Are you okay?"

"Shhh!" said Donald. "Not too loud. We don't want to scare him away this time!"

The scratching grew more persistent as Bill sat up and stared at the window, his eyes wide open now.

"Wake Mr. Clarke," added Donald. "He'll know what to do."

Bill looked stunned, lost in the realization of what was happening, as he swung his feet around, reached down on the floor, and nudged their sleeping host.

"Don't say anything," whispered Bill, "but we've got a visitor outside."

"Incredible," said George, whispering back as he raised himself up on his elbows. "I thought I heard him in the trees when we changed cars, but we were driving seventy ... eighty miles an hour to get here. I can't believe he kept up with us the whole time."

"What do we do?" said Donald.

George stood, trying to think. He went to the kitchenette, then opened the refrigerator door and took out an apple.

"He hasn't eaten in days, I'll bet," he replied—distressed by the notion. "This oughta do the trick. Don't make any fast moves. ... Donny, hide the shoes under the bed in case he tries to fight us for them."

George went to the front door and opened it just as Donald shoved the old shoebox out of sight, followed by his own Silver Shoe wrapped up in his jacket.

An instant later, they heard a flapping noise outside.

George peered into the night air. He stood in silence under the yellow light and waited.

"I know you're out there," he whispered after a moment. Then he leaned over the second-floor railing that ran the length of the building and scanned the entire area, mindful not to wake his neighbors as he continued. "I know who you are and why you're here. There's no need to be frightened. Come have something to eat with us."

He waited a few seconds longer, but there was still no response.

Then he closed his eyes.

As painful as this was going to be, George understood he would have to recall his past now in order to make the connection.

He took a deep breath.

"I knew another from your world, years ago," he began with stoic caution. "*Kibbero*. ... I met him when I was a boy."

A long silence followed before George turned toward the apartment door and shrugged.

"It's no use," he said.

A moment later, he heard the loud flapping again and spun back around.

Sitting across from him, perched on the railing, was a large flying monkey with dark brown fur. The monkey blinked at him with a curious expression, then ruffled his wing feathers and shivered involuntarily from the cold.

George took a deep breath and reached his hand out with the apple.

"Here, take this," he said.

The monkey stared at it, then looked into George's eyes, then back at the apple. He seemed to be studying them both, trying to make up his mind.

Finally he reached across, grabbed the apple from George's hand, and bit into it.

"Thank you," he said in a gruff, peculiar voice after swallowing his first bite.

"You must be cold," said George.

The monkey nodded and took another bite.

Donald and his father stood in the doorway with their mouths gaping open at this astounding creature.

"You have what does not belong to you," said the ape with a growl as his eyes fixed on Donald.

"Yes," replied the boy, trembling a bit.

"Quick, come inside," said George. "We can't let anybody see us."

The Gardners retreated into the apartment as George waited by the door. He held it open, but the creature didn't move.

"We're not going to hurt you," said George. "In fact, I think we can help you get home. Please ... come inside so we can talk."

The flying monkey finished his apple, tossing the core with wild abandon over the railing. He sat for a moment, eyeing George. Then Donald emerged in the doorway again with a nervous grin, clutching a half-empty bag of French fries. He pulled one from the bag and placed it in the palm of his hand. The monkey sniffed the air and hopped off the railing as Donald backed slowly into the apartment while the monkey followed him inside this time.

George closed the door behind them and turned a light on as Donald surrendered his bag of fries to their hungry visitor.

"You knew my grandfather?" said the creature between bites.

George was thrown for a moment and stammered.

"Yes," he replied. "Kibbero ... he was your *grandfather*?"

"What became of him?" said the monkey.

"I'm not sure," said George, and he could feel himself growing anxious again. For a half-century, he had tried to block these memories from his mind or at least come to grips with them. Now he was going to have to talk about them openly.

Perhaps it was for the best.

He allowed his thoughts to drift back to a distant, more innocent time of his youth.

"He lived in our barn for about two weeks," began George. "There was a—"

"Why did you not give him what he came for?" the monkey interrupted.

"Because I was *scared*," said George all of a sudden. "I was just a kid, and I couldn't believe the things he was telling me about Oz and the Silver Shoes. It was so incredible."

"Why would he tell *you* such things?" said the monkey with another growl.

"Shhh! Please," whispered George, pleading with him. "We can't let anyone hear us." He took a deep breath, then forged ahead. "I owe you the truth ... for your grandfather's sake," he added, nodding to confirm his decision. "I will tell you what happened."

"I will listen, then," the monkey replied.

"I trapped Kibbero in our barn when he first came looking for the shoe ... and after a while, I got him to say many things. I brought him food and water and made sure he had warm blankets at night and was hidden safe from harm. In exchange, he told me about Oz and his life there. I kept his feet tied with a rope to a wooden post so he couldn't get away, but he still had plenty of room to move about and walk. ... I made him as comfortable as possible, and I got a feeling from his reaction that I was showing him the first kindness he'd seen in a long time. When I finally took my mother and father down to the barn to meet him, they were upset and frightened. They wanted to call the police and have him taken away, but I talked them out of it. I almost turned him loose myself right then—and I *would* have, too, except I was afraid he still might hurt us."

"Why did you not give him what he came for?" repeated the monkey. "He would have left you alone, then."

"Because he told me how powerful that shoe was," said George. "How dangerous it might be if it ended up in the wrong hands. After Kibbero explained this, I knew it wasn't right just to hand over the shoe. It was clear that only the cruelest of masters would have sent him on such a *pitiless* mission between worlds—and I wasn't about to surrender a powerful weapon like that to such a vile manipulator. After a while, I began to realize your grandfather was hoping I would feel this way. He never said it, and I don't even think he could have put it into words, but in his own way, I believe he was warning me not to give him the shoe."

"Impossible," said the monkey. "He was bound by his master's command to return to Oz with the Silver Shoe."

"Yes, I know that," said George. "And if I had released him right then, he would have done everything he could to take it away from me. But I don't believe he told me all he knew about the Silver Shoes and their powers just because I had him tethered to a post. I saw it in his eyes ... and I swear to you—he was warning me not to let him finish his task." George looked down for a moment, then continued. "Over the years, I've grown to respect Kibbero for his bravery. He made the ultimate sacrifice to help others. You see, without that shoe, he had no way of getting home again. Kibbero shared the history of the shoes and told me about the quest for them in the Land of Oz—but neither of us was aware of the Wizard's secret society or the underground agency that were both here in this world searching for them as well."

The monkey cocked his head.

"You know the Wizard?" he said, sounding surprised. "Where is he now?"

"No ... I don't know him," said George. "He's been dead for years. But he has disciples hidden among us who have made it their goal to get their hands on the shoes."

"What became of my grandfather?" asked the monkey again.

George braced himself for the difficult answer.

"Word got out that we had a *curiosity* living with us in our barn," he began. "It started as idle gossip. A few neighbors stopped by to have a look. Two older women even fainted dead away when they first laid eyes on him—which made me laugh, come to think of it."

George smiled at the recollection before his thoughts turned dark again.

"Then the news began to spread ... and I'll never forget the day I saw a dozen cars and those three white trucks driving up the dirt road, out by our field. I knew it wasn't going to be good. So I ran inside the house and took the shoe from its hiding place. Then I hid around the corner from the barn, next to a tall stack of hay, and I waited to see what would happen."

George paused as he felt a lump rise in his throat.

"I watched, helpless to do anything, as Kibbero was *caged* by a group of government agents. They marched into our barn wearing their clinical white coats and hauled him away in one of those scientific trucks. He looked so scared, and I could hear him screaming. I wanted to stop them, but I was just a boy. Two other men in dark suits stood with my parents, giving them strict orders not to discuss this with anyone. My mother was in shock, and I could hear more people inside the house, tearing it apart. Everyone seemed preoccupied at the moment, so I made up my mind right then to escape with the shoe. It's funny, the decisions we make in a split-second that alter everything. ... So I took off through the north field."

He lowered his gaze again and paused.

"I had no idea I would spend the rest of my life running away from them," he added.

"So many lives ruined by these shoes," said the monkey.

George looked up. There were tears in his eyes this time.

"I want to put a stop to it," he said. "I want to *end* this."

"Then give me the shoes," said the monkey. "I will take them back to Oz right now, and your problem will be solved."

"I can't do that," said George with polite resistance. "You know I can't."

"What are we to do, then?" said the monkey. He blinked several times, followed by a discouraged sigh. "We are all lost."

"Yes," added Bill. "I know you have a plan. Please, George ... tell us what you've got in mind."

"Donny, would you hand me my jacket?" he replied, pointing to the armchair.

Donald turned to find Mr. Clarke's coat draped over the back of the chair, and he gave it to him. George reached into the front pocket and took out an old, yellowed envelope. He opened it with care and removed several frail pieces of paper. Clearing his throat, he began to read from them:

My dear friend,

If you are reading this letter, we are both very fortunate, indeed. It means that my last will and testament has been carried out successfully, and it is also safe to assume you have in your possession at least <u>one</u> of the legitimate Silver Shoes of Oz.

That's right, my friend, Oz is a real place ....

"What is that?" asked Bill, frowning.

"A handwritten letter from L. Frank Baum," replied George. "It arrived at our farm about a week after I tried the shoe on."

"I don't understand," said Bill. "Mr. Baum was long dead by then, wasn't he?"

"He passed away in 1919," said George with a nod, "and I have no idea how I got this or who sent it to me—or even how they came to learn I had the shoe. I can only guess this letter was held by one of his confidants or relatives in good faith. Perhaps it was a guarded family secret, handed down from generation to generation. I may never know the truth—but it came addressed to me on the farm, just the same."

"Did my grandfather learn of this letter?" said the monkey.

"I read it to Kibbero as soon as it arrived," said George. "He was good enough to explain some of the more obscure references to Oz. And for whatever reason, we hadn't realized, until that moment, that others beyond our area were also aware of the shoe. We pored through this letter in the barn that day, and that's when we began to understand—"

There was a loud knock at the front door, and everyone froze.

"Mr. Peters?" said a voice belonging to an elderly woman. "It's Mrs. Kennedy."

"The building manager!" whispered George. He looked at the flying monkey who seemed agitated now. "Get him out of sight, and don't say a word!"

Donald and Bill scooted the bewildered creature around the corner, past the kitchenette doorway, and into the bathroom. George waited just long enough, then cracked the front door open.

"I'm so sorry, Mrs. Kennedy," he said, leaning his head out with a humble smile. "Were we disturbing you?"

"Not only me, Mr. Peters," she replied with a sour expression. "You've woken up half the building. My telephone's rung three times in the last fifteen minutes. Honestly, Bob, this is not like you."

"I've got visitors from out of town," said George. "I guess I'm not used to having them. We weren't thinking. I'm sorry you had to trouble yourself, and I promise we'll keep it down."

"You've always been such a quiet man," she continued. "I hope things aren't changing now."

"No, of course not," he said with cheerful assurance. "In fact, we're all leaving this morning for a trip."

"Well ... fine, then," she answered with a nod. George noticed she was staring at him in a curious way. "But please try to be more considerate," she added.

"Absolutely, Mrs. Kennedy."

George closed the door again and a moment later fell against it, breathing a sigh of relief as Donald, his father, and the monkey emerged from the bathroom.

"We've got to get out of here before we're discovered," he whispered with renewed purpose.

"Mr. ... *Peters?*" said Donald mockingly.

"You don't think I use my real name around here, do you?"

"I must know more!" said the monkey, trying hard to remain quiet. He hopped up onto the seat of the armchair, bobbing his head up and down with anticipation. "What will happen now?"

"We're leaving for Dorothy McCollum's old farmhouse in Kansas," said George.

"*Dorothy?*" repeated the monkey in disbelief. "You know of the child Dorothy from Kansas? The brave little girl who came to Oz?"

"Yes—I'll explain more when we get there," said George as he put his jacket on. "You can keep up with us, can't you? You've managed to do a terrific job of it so far."

"I will follow you," said the monkey. "That, you may depend on."

"Won't you get caught?" said Donald, sounding concerned. "I mean, it'll be daylight soon. People could see you then."

"The people of your world seldom look up," stated the monkey. "And the ones who do don't understand what they see."

Donald laughed. "They probably just think you're a big scary bird."

"They believe what they choose to believe," added the monkey.

"All right, my friend," said George, chuckling as he put his hand on their new comrade's shoulder. "I promise I'll help you as best I can. I owe that much to your grandfather."

"You may call me Anirbas," said the monkey, and he bowed respectfully to George.

"Nice to know you, Anirbas—I'm George Clarke," he replied with a smile, and he bowed himself in return.

George stepped outside the apartment after that, making sure the coast was clear. He peered over the edge of the walkway, then gestured for Anirbas to join him. The monkey hopped up onto the railing with cautious restraint, spread his impressive wings, and took flight into the darkness.

Donald collected both of the Silver Shoes and his jacket from their short-lived hiding place under the bed while Mr. Gardner filled the empty McDonald's bags with fruit, potato chips, almonds, and other assorted snacks from the refrigerator.

Moments later, the threesome made their way quietly down to the deserted street and drove off into the early morning stillness.

Chapter Eleven

ELLIE REACHED THE bottom of the spiral staircase and stopped. Standing alone for a minute, she trembled in the darkened alcove. Fear had won out as she listened to the powerful voices that echoed around her.

"*... for the good of mankind. Ruler of worlds, both civilized and uncivilized,*" they proclaimed with unified zeal. And this time, their chosen language was English. "*Provider of power. Instiller of life. Protector of the Original Enchantment. He shall bestow the Three Gifts of infinite Wisdom, steadfast Bravery, and profound Compassion on us all. Even in death shall he lead us to an eternal life, free from disease, free from despair, and free from want. In the jeweled city, he shall rise again to sit upon the throne ....*"

She emerged from the alcove, then peered around the corner of the garden wall. From what she could tell, an enormous religious celebration was taking place just beyond the expansive courtyard, through a pair of golden doors that stood over forty feet high. They were propped open now, beckoning her to come inside.

Ellie scanned the area for any sentinels patrolling the grounds and spotted one right away, stationed in the garden. He was dressed like the others with his long brocade robes and green-tinted glasses, and he was carrying a rifle.

Another was positioned high up on the surrounding wall overlooking the courtyard. He wasn't much of a threat, however, leaning against the stone balustrade, fast asleep.

The man in the garden crossed to a small bench and took a seat. Moments later, he set his rifle down with a disinterested yawn, bent forward, and put his head in his hands.

Ellie decided to make her move then. She advanced with care into the courtyard and kept a keen eye about her as she progressed down a path of yellow bricks surrounding the grounds that led straight to the golden doors on the opposite side.

All at once, it hit her as she stared at her feet.

"*We believe in Oz, the Great and Terrible,*" they roared with passion. "*Slayer of all witches. Father of all sorcerers. Benevolent Wizard of the four countries, the land beyond the Shifting Sands, and the world beyond the Original Enchantment. Oz, the giver of life. ... Oz, the warrior of truth. ... Oz, the rightful sovereign of all living things ....*"

Ellie gazed at the expert masonry of the Yellow Brick Road beneath her feet.

Her wildest thoughts had proven true. These poor misguided souls were worshipping the Wizard of Oz, a character from a *children's* book—following him blindly as if he were a real person! It didn't seem possible in this day and age.

She was misunderstanding them. She *must* be. A mental fog had impaired her judgment due, no doubt, to nervous exhaustion. This was clearly a grand, glorious, and terribly *funny* hallucination.

But it wasn't a mirage ... and it wasn't amusing either.

This was happening in front of her eyes.

Her mind ran through all she knew about these people. She thought of the large painting of the Emerald City, of Olive's green glasses and her book, even her *name*. It was a simple acronym. Both she and Zeller had names beginning with the letters O and Z.

Ellie recalled that the witch's shoes in the original story were not made of rubies, but rather forged out of *silver*.

Their fascination with her most cherished collectible had become all too obvious now as she arrived undetected in the doorway and stared at what appeared to be over a thousand human beings, all chanting in unison—row upon row, hands joined together, sitting with regal bearing in distinctively carved mahogany seats that encircled the walls of the great hall.

Each member of this unlikely congregation wore a pair of the little round spectacles. Their emerald lenses shimmered and danced throughout the crowd like the expressionless glass eyes of a thousand dolls.

In the center of the arena was a large platform with two life-sized golden statues, their faceless figures raised high, positioned imperially on two giant marble pedestals. They were dressed in vintage apparel, tailored from actual fabric—costumes from a bygone era, she thought. The taller of the two wore a dark gentleman's coat and top hat while the other had on a little girl's prairie dress and pinafore.

Suddenly Ellie understood. These were the idealistic likenesses of Dorothy and the Wizard, crafted of gold and clad in antique relics from a fictional past.

She continued at a steady pace through the doorway, her eyes wide with curiosity as she ventured into the arena, almost as if in a dream.

She kept moving toward the golden idols until she spotted an elderly man on the platform in front of them. He noticed her as well and froze, pointing a finger at her.

All eyes in the great hall turned to face her in horror.

Within seconds, the congregation fell silent. She heard nothing but the sound of her own beating heart.

"We have a visitor!" said the old man, breaking the pause. His voice echoed in the stadium.

Ellie was flanked by two guards. They grabbed her by the arms.

The old man gasped.

"*Olive?* What is the meaning of this?" he shouted in anger.

"I was about to ask you the same thing," she replied, summoning enough nerve to raise her voice in defiance.

A guard reached over and pulled the green glasses from her face.

Then the old man's expression softened as he stepped back with outstretched arms.

"This is indeed a rare moment for us all! It's *Mrs. Eleanor Gardner,* ladies and gentlemen!" he announced in awe. "This is the woman who discovered one of the Silver Shoes of Oz!"

The crowd reacted with audible gasps. Some chattered away, followed by a spontaneous round of applause. Their enthusiasm escalated as the full congregation rose to its feet with a rapturous ovation.

Ellie stared back at them, utterly speechless.

"It just doesn't make sense to me," Bill blurted out after they had been on the freeway for about an hour.

There had been an unsettling silence in the car up to that point.

"Why do we have to take the shoes back to Dorothy's farm?" he continued as his restless eyes studied the road ahead. They were beginning to see the first glimpses of a sunrise in the east. "We're not going to just toss them through a portal and walk away, are we? I assume it's not so easy to locate one of those. Besides, who or even *what* would end up with them after that?"

George nodded as he attempted to sort through this sudden stream of questions.

"You're right," he replied. "I was trying to explain it when Mrs. Kennedy showed up—and I wanted Anirbas to hear it, too. In truth, it doesn't have much to do with the location of a portal."

Donald frowned. "Then why did you say it did before?"

"Because I needed you to come with me, and I couldn't risk jeopardizing this mission if you refused. I'm afraid you still might change your minds once you hear what's in store for us."

Bill shook his head. "It's not enough that I want my wife back so badly I've honored every request you've made of us so far?" he said with a glare.

"The answer's in your letter, isn't it?" said Donald suddenly.

George smiled with admiration. "You don't miss a trick, do you? Mr. Baum reveals more in this one letter than he does in all of his books or agency reports. Unfortunately anyone who finds the shoes is saddled with the burden of this information—and Baum issues us a grave warning."

"What does he say?" asked Donald.

George hesitated. "I wasn't sure you should know about this yet, in the event we come up empty-handed when we get to the farm. It would be a great disappointment to you both."

Bill shrugged. "I have no idea what my expectations are anymore—about *anything*."

"Good point," said George, grinning. "All right, here goes. ... In his letter, Frank describes a secret language of Oz called *Mohepkti*."

"What is ... Mohepkti?" repeated Donald, working hard to pronounce the word.

"Only the most powerful witches and sorcerers even dare to mention it by name. It was forbidden hundreds of thousands of years ago. ... It's the language that first enchanted the Land of Oz."

"*That's* what's carved all over the shoes!" said Donald.

"Right again," said George in awe of the boy's understanding.

"And the voices in my dream. *That* was Mohepkti, too," he added.

George nodded.

"But how do I know these things?" said Donald.

"How, indeed," replied George. "I don't fully understand what has happened to us myself, but I can tell you this much—we both possess a fraction of the knowledge that can be gained by wearing the shoes. We came to *know* things because we tried one on. For example, we know those markings mean something important."

"I knew all along it was writing," said Donald as his eyes fixed ahead in a steady gaze. "I guess I've always known that it was ... instructions."

"Exactly!" shouted George, attempting to contain his enthusiasm. "The shoes themselves tell us how to use them. They act as a gateway to the fundamental life force that created Oz. Picture what it would be like if you could conjure the skies or the oceans or the earth just the way you want them, out of nothing at all—or if you could generate life itself and remove it again at will.

Dorothy wore both shoes for days on her journey to the Emerald City. Imagine the breadth of knowledge she acquired during that time. Only someone with the simplicity and innocence of a *child* could resist the temptation to use their dark magic. In the end, when all other options had failed her, Dorothy did call upon it to bring her home again, under the guidance of a wise and benevolent sorceress."

"But how does that tie in with our trip to the farm?" said Bill.

"I'm afraid we only have a piece of the puzzle, gentlemen," said George. "Baum describes this ancient language and explains how it's been used in the past to command the shoes—but he doesn't teach us any of the words. It would be too great a risk, especially if his letter ended up in the wrong hands."

"So what does he say we should do with the shoes?" asked Donald.

"Both Baum and Dorothy are begging us to destroy them if they should ever be found," he replied in a sober tone.

"I would think that was impossible from everything you just told us," said Bill. "Can they actually be destroyed?"

"Nothing we know of has that much power," said George in agreement, "with one obvious exception—the shoes themselves."

"Self-destructive!" shouted Donald.

"A spell can be performed while wearing them that will destroy the Silver Shoes forever," added George.

"Mr. Clarke ... I've *seen* Oz," said Donald all of a sudden.

His father turned to him with an astonished look.

"I know you have," said George, smiling.

"I can still remember what it looks like from my dream," said the boy. "It was beautiful but scary, too—not like our world is."

"Our world is frightening in *different* ways," said George, deep in thought. "I've wanted to see Oz again myself," he continued with a touch of regret. "But those dreams fade in time. Now, after more than fifty years ... it's hard to remember."

"George, you've known about this destruction spell all along," said Bill. "Why didn't you use it on your own shoe?"

"For starters, I didn't know the right words to say."

"But you could have put the shoe on again and figured them out, right? I mean, it would have come to you eventually," said Bill.

"I wasn't in any hurry to do that," replied George. "Aside from the prospect of being *hunted* again like a wild animal, the idea of wearing a Silver Shoe even for an instant was fairly disturbing. It's hard to describe, but during those brief, intense moments of connection, I was taken to a very dark place, way down inside me. I haven't exactly been eager to go back there again. Dorothy was extremely brave to keep them on her feet for so long, I can tell you that much. Maybe the idea of facing a horrible witch without any additional defenses was an even worse prospect. As it turns out, I avoided the decision until it was too late. After months of being a *kid fugitive* on the run, I finally worked up enough courage to give it one more try. That's when I discovered I had outgrown the shoe. It was a relief at the time—but over the years, it's been a source of frustration and deep regret. I've kept the shoe hidden, guarded safely for half a century now, and I've learned some incredible things from wearing it the one time. But I will never have the knowledge required for a spell of that magnitude. It's just as well. Baum wrote in his letter that one shoe alone wouldn't likely be powerful enough for a charm like that. So I've waited more than fifty years, hoping against all hope that a second shoe might turn up within my lifetime."

"It's hard to believe," said Bill in a hush, "with so little chance of this working out, why did Mr. Baum even bother to write this letter and arrange for it to be delivered, long after his death?"

"Because *he* believed," said George. "Dorothy McCollum and Frank Baum never gave up hope that people like us would be the ones to find the shoes. Their steadfast, irrational commitment is what has kept me going all these years."

"But if we don't know the words to say, what can we do about it?" said Bill.

Donald beamed. "They're hidden at the farmhouse!"

"My dear young friend, you've come to learn so much in such a short amount of time," said George. "Frank and Dorothy wrote the spell on a piece of paper and locked it inside an antique ivory box. They buried it four feet beneath the dirt floor of an old tool shed on the McCollum farm ... and I only hope that after all this time, we can still find it there."

"Why didn't you dig the box up yourself when you first learned about it?" said Bill. "Why wait until now?"

"That farm has been under constant surveillance for over a century," replied George. "Between the Order of the Wizard and government agents combing the area for shreds of information, I couldn't get near the place unless I had to. Besides, I had one shoe and couldn't perform the spell even if I retrieved that box. But we have *both* shoes with us now—and no other choice. It's a risk we've got to take."

"Will there be trouble once we get there?" asked Bill, sounding nervous again.

"No living person knows about this box," said George with as much confidence as he could muster. "There isn't any reason to suspect we'd be heading out there now to dig it up. We're only ten minutes away—and I doubt we'll find armed guards waiting for us at this hour."

Donald cringed. "Will we have to say those chanting words when we dig it up?"

"Not we, Donny," he replied. *"You."*

A stunned silence followed.

"But ... but why do I have to do it alone?" said Donald.

"I won't let him," said Bill. "It's too dangerous!"

"Do you want to have your wife back again?" said George with a blunt stare. "Mrs. Gardner's safe return is part of this plan. I don't see any other way to accomplish it. Believe me, I would do this myself, but I'm too old now."

"Then *I'll* do it," said Bill. "I'm willing to take the risk, but Donny, he ... he's just a boy!"

"You don't understand," said George, trying to curb his frustration. "We don't fit the shoes. Your son is the only one who can do this."

"You mean he'll have to put them on?" stammered Bill. "All those evil witches and sorcerers will see him again! You said so yourself!"

"We'll have to act quickly, I agree—but Donny will have more power than any sorcerer or witch in Oz."

"What good is it having that much power if you don't know how to *use* it?" said Bill, nearly in a rage now. "He could never hold his own against them!"

"There's a *reason* why they haven't come here themselves to get the shoes," said George. "There's *got* to be—or they would have invaded our world long ago."

"Look, even if these supernatural invaders don't show up personally, that won't stop them from sending additional pawns to do their bidding," shouted Bill. "You have no idea what could happen if Donny is discovered wearing the shoes!"

George was silent. The enormity of their mission was overwhelming him as well.

"It's true, I don't know what could happen," he replied as he took a deep breath and contemplated further. The responsibility of fifty years was taking its toll on him. "At least we have history on our side," he added after harnessing what little energy he had left. "Here's what we've established so far—*someone* in Oz discovered the location of the first Silver Shoe a half-century ago when I was a boy, and the most we got back was a single flying monkey, transported here without sufficient means to retrieve it and no way of getting home again without stealing it back first. The same thing happened to Donny a few days ago when he tried the second shoe on. Again, a search party of *one* was sent here with the same order and the same inadequate means to carry it out."

"Maybe their masters were just being careful not to get caught," said Donald.

"I wouldn't second-guess another world's strategy," said his father.

"I'm sure I don't understand their philosophy or their limitations either," said George in agreement, "but since this search-and-rescue approach has been attempted twice already, I believe it could be the same master with the Golden Cap both times. If so, there is only one command left, at most, before the cap becomes useless to him. This master, powerful as he or she may be in the Land of Oz, is running out of effective resources in our world. I'd stake my life on it—and it's an advantage we've got to take."

"Dad ... I'll do it," announced Donald suddenly. "I'm not scared. And I know you both would do this yourselves if you could ... so if it will make things right again, I'd like to try."

His father looked away and closed his eyes in defeat.

"Donny ... I will tell you what little I know about commanding the shoes," said George with a respectful nod. "Kibbero taught me a variation to the Traveling Spell. It's based on the chant you heard in your dream ... the same spell that was supposed to bring him home again if he were ever holding onto a Silver Shoe."

"The *what* spell?" asked Donald with an eager smile.

"Traveling Spell," repeated George. "Kibbero saw it performed several times in Oz, and he memorized the forbidden text. It works in our world with just one shoe," he added. "That's how I was able to avoid getting caught by the feds back in Iowa. But you don't want to do it the way Baum describes in his book, and you have to be very careful—use it only if you absolutely *have* to."

"Look, I've already told you I have no idea where they were headed," said Mrs. Kennedy as she paced the floor of her modest apartment, still wearing curlers and a blue flannel bathrobe. She was beginning to regret her impulsive phone call to the police. "It's just that I've been watching that alert on TV all night long, and I couldn't help but think that from the *sketch* they keep showing ...." She hesitated, then changed the subject. "Are you sure you wouldn't like some coffee?"

"No—thank you," replied Banning with a polite gesture.

"I really didn't see who was with Mr. Peters tonight," she continued. "Maybe I'm wrong about the whole thing. ... I'm sure I am," she added apologetically.

"It's all right, Mrs. Kennedy," said Banning with an encouraging smile. "You did the right thing by calling us. Any information you have now would be helpful."

"Well, I probably wouldn't have troubled you at all if Bob hadn't roused half the building at four in the morning. I was standing in his doorway, handing him a lecture about the noise, and it suddenly occurred to me how much he resembled that sketch they keep showing on television. I couldn't stop thinking about it. Oh, I'm sure it's only my imagination."

"How long have you known Bob Peters?" asked Lamont.

"Ever since he moved in," she said. "Eight or nine years now. He's a quiet, polite man—*normally*, that is. Always keeps to himself. I don't know much about him, come to think of it. But he pays his rent on time and doesn't complain like some of the others do. He's no trouble at all, really."

"I wonder if you wouldn't mind taking a look at this," said Banning as he reached into his pocket and removed a faded photograph.

Mrs. Kennedy took the weathered snapshot and walked over to an end table to pick up her reading glasses. Then she held the picture up to the light.

"This isn't very recent," she said with a sniff. "Taken some time ago, wasn't it? Where did you get it?"

"Does the man look familiar?" said Lamont.

"It's Mr. Peters, all right," she replied with a nod. "No mistaking that. His hair's a lot darker and fuller here, but it's definitely him."

"Thank you, Mrs. Kennedy," said Banning as he returned the photo to his pocket and gestured with an expression of overwhelming dismay to his partner. "After all these years ... our Mr. *Clarke* turns up under our noses!"

"I'm on it," said Lamont, taking out his cell phone. "You don't think they're heading to the *farm* now, do you?"

"They've got both shoes with them," replied Banning. "There's no telling what could happen—but the farm is the first place we've got to look. Make sure everyone understands this is not a drill. We're going to need plenty of backup!"

"What's happening?" stammered Mrs. Kennedy, alarmed by their behavior. "Is everything all right?"

"Ma'am, we can't thank you enough for your call," said Lamont as they made their way to the front door. "You've been a great help!"

Chapter Twelve

GEORGE SLOWED THE car and pulled it to the shoulder of the freeway. In the early morning haze, he could see an empty field of tall grass with a few scattered elms in the distance. Further off, there were more trees clustered together in a long row, but not a soul was in sight. Just miles of empty, gray quiet.

"Why are we stopping here?" asked Donald.

"Because we've arrived," said George. "This is it."

He turned the ignition off and got out of the Toyota. Donald and his father exchanged uneasy glances before they followed him.

They stood together in silence for a moment, examining their surroundings, while Donald clutched the old shoebox. He shivered suddenly and zipped up his jacket.

George moved to the back of the car, then opened the trunk, took out an old shovel, and closed it again.

He pointed across the field.

"See over there beyond that oak tree? See the windmill?"

On the far side of the field was an insignificant iron structure with crude, rusty blades fanning out at the top, no longer able to rotate on their own.

"If you hadn't said something, I would have missed it," said Bill.

"I guess I thought there would be a farmhouse," added Donald, somewhat disappointed.

"That's been gone for years now," replied George.

Donald nodded. "I remember ... you told us."

"No one's lived on this land for over a century," George continued. "The government took ownership of this whole stretch of property that runs parallel to the freeway. They've had it for some time now, and they won't build anything on it, as you might have guessed. So here it sits, fading away a little more with each passing year."

"When was the last time you saw it?" asked Bill.

"About ten years ago," said George. "I borrowed a friend's car and stole a quick peek from this very spot. A section of the barn was still standing back then."

Suddenly George started walking toward the old windmill with great purpose.

Bill and Donald followed him into the grass.

"Is this really where *Dorothy* used to live?" said the boy after a moment. He was doing his best to keep up with the two grown men and their hurried gait. "This is where everything happened?" he added, out of breath.

"That's right," said George, grinning. He was amused by Donald's repetitive questions, but he understood the reason for them. Even with the barn and farmhouse missing, there was an elusive sense of wonder in the air—a mystical quality lingering from a century ago.

They continued for another minute without saying a word before George stopped again and pointed.

"If you look over there on the ground, you can still make out traces of the stone foundation where their first farmhouse used to be."

"I never thought I would wake up one day," said Mr. Gardner in amazement, "and discover that a story from my childhood ... one of those marvelous, incredible fairy tales ... was true."

"I understand what this means to you, Bill, believe me," said George. "But there's work to be done," he reminded them both. "I'm afraid we're running out of time."

Beyond the windmill, they began to see a plain wooden structure, long and rectangular in shape. The wood was faded with splintered gaps along the boards, and a door was hanging by a single rusty hinge on one side.

"Is that the old tool shed?" said Donald.

"That's it," replied George. "And I only hope we can find the ivory box now."

They moved past the windmill and were no more than twenty feet from their destination ...

... when a man wearing a dark, full-length overcoat stepped out from behind the shed, looking like an ordinary businessman, well-dressed and in his mid-forties.

He was smiling, pointing a handgun directly at them. George could see he had an antique ivory box with traces of dirt clinging to it, clutched under his arm.

"Welcome, my friends," he said. "I was worried you weren't going to make it, but I'm quite pleased to see that you have. I'll keep the introduction brief. My name is Owen Zeller, and I've come to collect the shoes."

"*Zeller?*" repeated Bill, gritting his teeth. "Where is my wife? What have you done with her?" He lunged forward as George held his arm out in restraint.

"Temper now," said Zeller with a playful frown, making a disapproving gesture with his gun. "Your wife is quite well, I assure you. We've exhausted our need for her. I will see that she is returned to you safely once I have the Silver Shoes."

"How did you know about the ivory box?" asked a devastated George.

"Why, the same way *you* did, Mr. Clarke," he replied, reaching into his pocket to remove a faded envelope. "It's unfortunate that you missed the delivery of this letter by just one day. Naturally I had it intercepted at the post office. It's addressed to your lovely *wife*, Mr. Gardner, although it appears to be from our not-so-recently departed Mr. Baum—incredible as that may sound. To my delight, it tells me everything I need to know about your destructive plans for these shoes."

"Two shoes, two letters," said George numbly.

"It stands to reason," said Zeller with a smile. "I assumed you'd be the logical recipient of a similar letter, Mr. Clarke, so when I came to learn late yesterday that it was *you* who had kidnapped the Gardners, well, that was a double dose of good fortune for me. It wasn't difficult to guess you'd be coming straight here after that."

"Where are the others?" said George, looking around. "Surely you didn't show up here by yourself."

Zeller waivered a bit. His eyes darted around.

"Ah, yes ..." he began. "Well, I thought it best that my colleagues didn't know about this happy turn of events just yet. In time, they will celebrate with me."

"Betraying your own people?" said George with a sneer.

They noticed the faint wail of police sirens in the distance just then. Zeller craned his neck to hear them.

"You're wasting valuable time, Mr. Clarke," he replied with a nervous twitch. "Now if you would be so kind as to hand over the shoes—"

"Not a chance," shouted Bill.

"I would rethink your position if I were you. My little helper here is pointed right at your son's heart. It would be quite effortless for me to pull the trigger."

"You wouldn't dare!" roared Bill.

"Is that an invitation?" said Zeller, brandishing his weapon in defiance. "We're out of time, and I need those shoes!"

George looked up at the sky in desperation as his mind raced, struggling to find a way to stop this from happening. He wasn't sure, but he thought he saw something approaching from high above. He quickly suppressed an expression of recognition.

"All right," he said in an attempt to sound humble. He even lowered his head for added believability. "You win. Donny, give this man what he wants."

"But, Mr. Clarke," said Donald with a gasp, "how can I do that?"

"Give this *weasel* the shoes," said George.

"I'm glad you understand the complexity of the situation," said Zeller with a smirk. "Let's have them now, shall we?"

Donald hesitated, then stepped forward, clutching the shoebox. The howling sirens were growing closer and seemed to be increasing in numbers. Donald trembled with tears in his eyes as he held the shoebox out, offering it to Zeller ...

... when a nondescript, dark shape swooped past them, showing incredible speed and precision, as it knocked Zeller to the ground with a terrific force. The gun and ivory box flew out in front of him, scattering several feet apart from each other in the grass.

"Anirbas!" shouted a delighted Donald as his father leapt for Zeller and pinned him to the ground.

"Get his gun!" Bill called out.

George scooped up the handgun and ivory box and backed away to a safe distance as Donald dropped down in the grass and yanked his sneakers off. He tossed them aside.

"Donny, no!" shouted his father.

"It's the only way, Dad!"

He removed the lid to the box, reached inside, and took out the Silver Shoes. They gleamed in the morning sunlight as Anirbas settled on the ground just a few feet away from him.

"Now it begins!" their new friend announced with keen anticipation as he folded his wings.

Without delay, Donald slipped the first one on, followed by the second.

There was a brief, numbing silence.

Nothing seemed to move.

Suddenly the earth around him started to tremble. Donald found himself standing in the center of a series of circular shockwaves spreading out rapidly through the rippling grass toward the horizon.

From their position on the freeway, Banning and Lamont identified the small red Toyota parked ahead on the shoulder of the road. Off to the right, the familiar rusty windmill and tool shed had just come into view when their car stalled.

"It died on us!" said Banning.

Lamont stared at his cell phone, waiting for their supervisor to answer a question. He discovered it was dead, too.

Banning did his best to steady the vehicle, which had lost both its power steering and power brakes, and he realized that all the sirens from the dozens of state patrol cars around them had been silenced as well.

He tried hard to avoid crashing into the other cars as they all fought to maintain control of the road.

In a matter of seconds, the sky turned a dark purplish color, and a strong wind began to rise around them.

"Look!" shouted Donald, pointing at the sky. His feet tingled with energy.

An enormous whirlpool of a cloud circled above the open field with an unnatural green light penetrating from its edges. The axis of the cloud began to dip down in a slow, forceful motion toward the ground below.

Several police cars on the freeway lost control, spinning around and flipping over during the chaos.

"Grab my hand!" yelled George as he tucked the ivory box under his arm. "Hurry, before it's too late!"

Donald moved next to him and took Mr. Clarke's free hand.

"Anirbas!" shouted Donald. Then he gestured for the monkey in the ripping, howling wind. "Dad! *Hurry!*"

Bill jumped up and fought his way to his son, freeing Zeller from the ground. He grabbed hold of Donald's other hand just as the ferocious, dark funnel touched down not more than a hundred yards from where they were standing. Anirbas cried out in fear, barely reaching the group in time as he clung to one of Bill's legs and shielded his eyes from the debris.

"Say the words, Donny!" yelled George. "Remember what I told you in the car!"

Blades of grass and splinters of wood whizzed by their heads, followed by several uprooted trees tumbling through the air.

The police cars and state patrol vehicles that had made it safely to a stop emptied out now as their frightened occupants took cover in nearby roadside ditches.

Donald's ears popped from the sudden enormous pressure change. He took a deep breath, closed his eyes, and began to speak with great authority.

"Mahnk-tanilooqut Kohlbivyosk Ahshki-nobkwoeardu-fiostahj! *Take us to the castle of the Order of the Wizard in Germany! Take us to my mother now!*"

Just as he finished the command, Zeller managed to crawl over, reach out, and grab hold of Donald's left foot as a blinding silver light exploded around them.

Chapter Thirteen

ELLIE SAT MOTIONLESS in the antique chair by the chamber window. She watched the castle's medieval shadows with a frozen fascination as they drifted over the treetops below, stretching outward toward the facing mountain range like a shady blanket being pulled yard by yard across the immense forest. She had been there for hours now ...

... or was it days? ...

... staring vacantly into the late afternoon sky.

After her shocking discovery in the great hall, she had been escorted back to the tower and assigned a new nurse.

No one had spoken to her since.

For a while, at least, she had been trapped inside an aching silence and her own disturbing thoughts. But as the afternoon extended into a bleak eternity, her mind went numb. She felt removed and hollow now, void of all thought and emotion, resigned to sit and wait for her judgment.

Suddenly the cold marble beneath her feet began to shake. She stood up.

Was her mind playing tricks on her?

She whirled around as the attending nurse sitting in the far corner cried out in fear.

The large crystal chandelier above their heads tinkled and swayed back and forth as a blinding silver light burst through the chamber.

Ellie moved away from the window just in time as it exploded outward, showering beveled glass with pieces of stone and metal, down from the tower and out over the hillside below.

She was certain this was a hallucination. She had been sitting so long she was beginning to see and hear things.

Very strange things, indeed.

As she gazed across the room into the faces of her husband, her son, two unfamiliar men, and what appeared to be a *flying monkey* with large feathered wings ... an alarm bell sounded in the distance.

She shook her head in total rejection of her senses.

"Mom?" said Donald, panting as he stood in front of her. He had never seen his mother look so gaunt before. "Mom, are you all right?"

"No, it can't be," she muttered. "I'm either losing my mind or this is a cruel joke."

"It's neither, Mrs. Gardner," said George with gentle assurance. "We've come to take you home."

Bill rushed forward and threw his arms around his wife, hugging her tightly as she stood frozen, unable to process what was happening.

"I don't understand," she whispered. Then a tear rolled down her cheek. "Where did you come from?"

"He's getting away!" shouted Anirbas. The agitated monkey flapped his wings and pointed to the door. "The wicked man is leaving us!"

"It can *talk?*" stammered Ellie. "No, it ... this can't be happening to ...."

Her eyes fluttered and her knees buckled as she went limp in her husband's arms.

It was only then that they realized Owen Zeller was in the castle with them.

In a state of paralyzed confusion, they observed the bewildered nurse and Zeller slipping through the chamber door. It slammed shut and locked behind them as the distant alarm bell continued to warn of their intrusion.

Then a strange wind picked up inside the chamber, coming from the massive opening where the lead-paned window had just been moments earlier. It whistled and spiraled around them with great force as the sky outside shifted to a deep reddish-purple hue.

"They've seen us again!" shouted George, looking worried. "As long as Donny is wearing those shoes, they're going to know where we are!"

Bill held Ellie close to him. "Can you get us out of here before another tornado hits—or something even worse?" he said.

"Sure, Dad," replied Donald. "Quick, everybody, gather around!"

They joined him in the center of the room again, each linking hands as they had done before.

"Everybody ready?" shouted Donald, scanning their eager faces. "Okay, here we go. *Mahnk-tanilooqut Kohlbivyosk Ahshki-nobkwoeardu-fiostahj!* Take us back to my house now!"

They held their collective breaths and waited for the expected explosion of light ...

... but nothing happened.

Donald's heart pounded as he turned to George in search of an answer.

"Maybe you didn't say it right," said Bill. "Try again!"

"No, Dad, I was careful! I *know* these words!"

"It isn't any good," said George, looking down at Donald's feet. "I don't understand how it could have happened, but he's missing a shoe."

They were stunned in horrific silence. Donald felt his stomach tighten as he gazed at a gleaming Silver Shoe on his right foot and a plain white sock on his left.

Something had gone terribly wrong.

"The wicked man with the war pistol has it!" said Anirbas after a moment. "He took this with him just now!"

"Are you sure?" said George.

The monkey nodded as he hopped out in front of them. "He placed the shoe inside his coat before he ran to the door. We *must* get this back now! We have to—"

Anirbas stopped and cocked his head to one side. His eyes grew wide as he listened. Then he began to screech and flap his wings in an unexpected fit of hysteria.

"It's all right, Anirbas," said George. "Calm down, and we'll think of something we—"

"No! You don't understand! They are coming!" he announced with a growl as he moved to the edge of the opening and peered out into the turbulent sky. "*All* of them are coming now!"

"Who is coming?" asked George.

"The Master has ordered us here to retrieve the shoes!" he replied.

Bill helped his semiconscious wife over to the bed.

"You mean the Winged Monkeys are coming *here*?" said Donald.

Anirbas nodded. "Their journey has already begun!"

He pointed to the swirling purple and green clouds forming over the distant mountain range.

"We're dealing with one *powerful* sorcerer," said George breathlessly, then he turned to the others. "This castle will soon be under attack. Donny, you've got to get out of here and try to find the other shoe."

"But I can't leave everyone trapped in this room!" he replied.

"You have no choice," said George, grabbing the boy by the shoulders and steadying him. "You're our only hope. Zeller is bound to return with plenty of help. The Traveling Spell didn't work because you only had one shoe. It isn't powerful enough to transport all of us at the same time, but you can use it yourself. *Trust* me. I've done it before."

"Where would he go?" said Bill, sitting down next to Ellie on the bed and taking her hand. She was breathing easier now and listening to their conversation.

A restless Anirbas suddenly spread his wings and let out a frantic screech. Then he rose high up in the chamber, circled around, and dove with swift precision through the opening and out into the wilderness beyond.

"No!" shouted Donald. He ran after his friend, stopping at the edge of the window. "Anirbas, come back!"

Donald watched the monkey gain speed and soar up over the treetops.

"Let him go!" said George. "He is bound by the *cap's* command now, not ours."

Donald stood in silence among the broken glass and chunks of stone scattered all around him. His heart was heavy.

"Will he turn and fight against us?" he asked.

"I hope not," said George. "We could have used his help."

"Keep your voices down," said Ellie with restraint. "There's an intercom system in this room, and they might be listening to every word you say."

George nodded in gratitude, then crossed and sat on the bed next to Donald's parents.

"Gather around," he whispered. "We don't have much time, and it looks like these walls have got big ears."

"It'll be all right," said Bill. He smiled at Ellie and stroked her hair. She attempted a smile herself as Donald joined the others.

The wind whipping around them certainly seemed loud enough to mask a quiet conversation, he thought.

"Donny, take the shoe off," said George.

"Why?" he asked, frowning.

"So they can't see you anymore."

Donald nodded, then reached down and removed the Silver Shoe. He clutched it to his chest.

"I'm sure Zeller can't fit into the other one," added George, "and he wouldn't know the Traveling Spell even if he could."

"But he heard me say those words," replied Donald.

"Only once," said George, "and I'd bet my life he can't repeat that spell after hearing it the one time."

"But he might give his shoe to someone else," said Bill. "Someone smaller. *They* would have the power, then."

"Who, *Zeller?*" said George with a chuckle. "Give up his shoe? I think we're safe there. Listen, we're going to have plenty of trouble just as soon as the Winged Monkeys get here. So, Donny, you've got to—"

The door to the chamber burst open, and a dozen men entered carrying guns. Zeller made his way through the ranks to the front. They were distracted as they gaped in awe at the cavernous opening where the window used to be.

"Time to get out of here, Donny," whispered George as he handed Donald the ivory box. "Good luck."

Then an unsettling thunder boomed in the distance as if the sky were cracking wide open. George jumped to his feet and blocked Donald from Zeller's view.

"Grab the child!" said Zeller, noticing the attempted diversion. "He's got the other shoe!"

The men advanced toward the bed.

"You have more important things to worry about, Zeller!" shouted George as he pointed through the opening. "Your castle is under attack from Oz! Take a look!"

Zeller and his henchmen froze as they stared into the swirling purple and green clouds that had formed over the facing mountain range.

Then an explosion of brilliant red light seeped through the center of the mass. From the glowing golden core of this terrifying new energy emerged a few black specs. Within seconds, there were hundreds of tiny moving flecks of darkness, spreading out like a sinister plague over the horizon. They behaved like a swarm of locusts at first as their numbers increased and scattered outward until several thousand of the menacing simians hovered in the air, advancing steadily toward the castle.

The hair stood up on the back of Donald's neck at this frightening, primal vision unfolding in front of him. It reached down and grabbed hold of his most basic fears. The flying monkeys in *The Wizard of Oz* had always scared him on television, though he never would have admitted it to anyone.

That was nothing compared to the vast army descending upon them now.

Zeller's men stood with their mouths open.

"Our two worlds meet at last," said their leader in a reflective tone.

"They're coming here to get the shoes," said George. "And I'd be plenty worried if I were you."

This distraction was just long enough for Donald to finish uttering the words that would remove him from the impending danger.

A small flash of silver light enveloped him, drawing everyone's attention from the window, and by the time Zeller realized what was happening, it was too late.

"No, it cannot be!" he cried out in agony. "We're letting him get away!"

Donald stood on the soft, cool grass at the bottom of a steep hill, just outside the castle in the valley below. Tall pine trees loomed all around him, towering toward the sky, and a narrow bubbling stream with craggy rocks wound its way among the massive trunks.

His heart thumped as he clutched the Silver Shoe in one hand and the ivory box in the other. He knew he couldn't go far and leave everyone to face this battle alone. Finding the missing shoe was important, but helping his parents and friends out of the immediate crisis was even more critical.

As he gazed above the trees and scanned his eyes across the castle's many turrets, he discovered a golden light emanating from the jagged opening—the very chamber where he had just been.

He looked away toward the distant mountains and saw the enormous swarm of flying monkeys as they approached, accompanied by a faintly disturbing chattering sound.

An icy chill ran through him.

"It's up to *me* now," he said to himself as he took a deep breath and gathered his strength to continue.

Then suddenly he stopped.

It occurred to him that this forest was familiar.

He took a few small steps inside the labyrinth of trees, and his eyes pored over these ominous woods.

What could it be?

Donald heard a splashing sound from the creek nearby when all at once his dream from the previous night rushed back into his mind with forceful clarity and he remembered everything.

He decided, without hesitation, to confront his unseen fear.

As he moved beyond the first few branches, a lump rose in his throat. One or two dead limbs cracked under his feet, startling him. He stopped for a moment to gather his wits, then continued. Several yards ahead, he rethought his hasty decision and glanced back just long enough to see the immense trunks surrounding him on all sides. No path to guide him safely to the hillside. No towering beacon to show him the way out.

Turning again, he saw a cold, flickering light ahead—the only illumination in these woods ... *exactly* as it had appeared in his dream, he thought.

The misty, gray glow penetrated his will, tempting Donald with a serene power that commanded him to draw near and reveal himself.

A sudden realization washed over him, and he knew what was up ahead. He had known for a long time now, even before his last dream, that this unfathomable moment would come.

The keeper of the Golden Cap was here ... in this world ... looking for the Silver Shoes.

Chapter Fourteen

"SO WHAT'S IT going to be, Zeller?" asked George with an anxious look. "I'd say you were outnumbered, wouldn't you?"

The frenzied roar from the far-off mountain range had risen to an alarming level. It was even possible to distinguish the detailed, simian forms of the flying monkeys as they moved ever closer to the castle.

George realized it was only a matter of minutes before the siege began.

"You underestimate me, Mr. Clarke," said Zeller with a smirk. "I'm disappointed in you." He turned to his men and raised his voice in a sudden rage. "Prepare for counterattack! Arm yourselves!

Mr. Zanier—tell the others to stand by until I give the signal to fire!"

One man standing near the door appeared stunned by the order, but he nodded and hurried from the chamber while the others moved to the cavernous opening and gazed through it in silence.

"*Arm* yourselves?" repeated George in shock. "You mean you'd actually shoot these creatures down?"

"Rest assured we will do whatever is necessary to see that the Wizard's prophecy is fulfilled," he replied. "We've waited far too long for this moment."

Zeller's followers seemed equally surprised by his merciless statement.

"Yes, but they're creatures of *Oz*," said George. "*Sacred* in the eyes of your Order!"

"That is true," said Zeller after a moment. Then he turned from the window and searched the faces of his comrades, only to discover a telling resistance in their eyes. He noticed it right away, as did George—but taking a deep breath, he proceeded with even greater conviction. "We *must* have assurance that everything will resolve according to the Wizard's plan. It is the *only way!*"

His men appeared to remember themselves and nodded in dutiful agreement.

Zeller inspected them once more, then spoke with enormous volume and authority. *"We must never lose sight of our goal!"*

Donald was closing in on the strange light when a sharp rustling sound came from the shadows in front of him. He fell back in horror.

"Who's there?" he called out.

A pair of leathery hands grabbed him by the shoulders and helped him to his feet.

"Mr. Donny, are you all right?" asked a familiar voice.

"Anirbas, it's *you!*" said Donald, greatly relieved as he brushed himself off with one hand while clutching the Silver Shoe and ivory box in the other. "I thought you left to join the others."

"That, I did," he said. "Take my hand and come with me. You must not go any further."

"Why?" said Donald. "I already know what's up there."

"*No*, Mr. Donny!" whispered Anirbas. "You do not know the danger that awaits you. We must go back. We must go *now!*"

"I'm not afraid of your master," said Donald.

"Then you are a terribly foolish boy," replied the monkey as he took hold of Donald's hand and began to pull him along. "He is the wisest, most cunning of all sorcerers—one of the *ancients*. A self-appointed king among our minions. Even without his magic, he has great knowledge and the experience of centuries to call upon. He will easily know how to anticipate and control a boy like you."

Anirbas led a reluctant Donald back to the hillside by the edge of the woods.

"What do you mean, 'without his magic?'" said the boy.

They stood for a moment, panting from exhaustion, until Anirbas caught his breath enough to respond.

"I began to realize that I am not so bound to the commands of the Golden Cap in this world."

Donald was stunned. "Are you sure?"

"Your world is entirely lacking in magic," he continued. "*Civilization* stands in its way. You have doubt and common sense here, which destroy all witchcraft and sorcery. The Land of Oz is not yet civilized and never has been. It was isolated under the original enchantment for this very reason."

"So you're not a slave to the Golden Cap anymore?" said Donald, somewhat confused.

"I would seize that shoe from you right now if I were not free to ignore the Master's bidding."

Then Donald remembered he was cradling it and clutched it even tighter.

"I don't understand why you still want it, then," said Donald. "How could I use it to do *anything* now?"

"The Silver Shoes were among the first and most powerful talismans forged in Oz," said Anirbas. "They were created out of darkness, born of the original Mohepkti incantations and brought into your world a mere century ago by an innocent female child—a young human named Dorothy. She was unaware of what she had done, oblivious to the boundaries and expectations of magic. For reasons unknown to the wisest among us, those shoes were able to uphold their considerable powers here." Anirbas grinned as he continued. *"Now* I am understanding how my grandfather's will was free and how he was able to help your Mr. Clarke. I am also understanding why he chose to do so."

"Do you think you could help him again? Would you help *all* of us now?" said Donald.

"The Winged Monkeys and I will do everything we can to assist you in destroying these shoes," he vowed. "They are evil, Mr. Donny. They consume all who call upon their magic and drive them into madness. I have seen it with my own eyes. So many souls withered, broken, and lost through the ages. Each time their magic is summoned, a sacrifice must be offered from within. Good trades with evil. Logic trades with lunacy. And as the craving to use the dark power increases, so does the price paid for calling upon it. There is no way out again, no hope of redemption. Our only chance for salvation is to destroy the shoes forever."

"We'll *do* it," replied Donald. "Fly up and tell your friends— explain to them that they don't have to take the shoes after all. Tell the Winged Monkeys to invade the castle anyway, attack Zeller and his followers, and keep them all busy—but they should leave my parents and Mr. Clarke *alone*. Can you do that?"

"With great pleasure, Mr. Donny, but what about *your* plans? How will you find the other shoe in time? The Master is here now, and he is looking for them just as you are!"

Donald hesitated. He gazed up at the churning skies, then down at his lone shoe again.

"Mr. Donny?" tried Anirbas once more. He seemed eager for the boy's response.

Finally Donald looked back at his trusted friend and smiled.

"I am going to do what I must do ... for all of us," he vowed.

Chapter Fifteen

AS DONALD WATCHED the flying monkey take flight and soar up into the sky, he turned toward the dense woods …

… and began to venture back into them.

"Forgive me, Anirbas, but I've got to do it," he whispered to himself with a sigh.

There was no time for cautious evaluation. He had to work fast.

Within moments, he saw the same mysterious glow in front of him as it flickered through a web of dark branches, guiding him closer to his destiny.

This time, he didn't hesitate. Instead, he forged ahead, clutching his shoe and the ivory box closer to his heart.

Soon he came upon an unexpected opening—and as the thick trees began to part, he could see the iridescent colorless shape of a willowy figure standing in the center of the clearing. It was hunched over what appeared to be a faded wooden pulpit, rising from the ground, born out of the great knotted roots of the old trees.

The figure was tall and lean, dressed in long, flowing, shroud-like robes with an armored collar forged of expertly tooled gold.

A single massive emerald hung from its neck like a regal king.

As Donald moved closer, he could tell this was a *man*—with an ancient, waxen, skeletal face. A thin layer of cadaverous skin covered his hairless head. It was almost translucent. Donald could see the intricate network of blue veins coursing through it with relentless purpose. His piercing eyes glowed a sickly yellowish green inside their deep-set sockets as he extended a crooked finger and curved it narrowly downward onto the enormous pages of a primitive, leather-bound book. He seemed to be consumed with his task, searching page after page with eager intensity, when all of a sudden his head snapped toward Donald.

His luminescent eyes fixed on the boy.

"So it has come to this," announced the Master in a slow, weary delivery. His words were filled with the dry dust of centuries. "You have forced me here to collect what is mine."

Donald was speechless.

"A *Silver Shoe*," the Master continued as his voice began to rise with greatness at the sight of it. "But where is the other?"

"It's … I … It's somewhere inside the castle," said the boy, almost unable to move.

"Bring the pair to me at once," replied the ancient man, "or you must die."

Donald was more frightened now than he had ever been in his life.

"Your family and friends will die with you," added the Master.

His response was followed by a low, threatening rumble through the woods.

"I … I can't," said Donald, still struggling to speak. "I don't know where the other one is."

"One shoe takes you to the other," he hissed. "Even a pathetic *fool* should expect this. You have worn these shoes yourself! Have you not come to know it?"

"Yes," he thought out loud. "I *do* know it."

Suddenly Donald understood exactly why he had returned to these woods.

"They belong to *me* now," said the Master. "I'm the only one who can appreciate them. And I will have them again for myself. Nothing will stand in my way this time."

"You don't have your powers here," said Donald, his knees nearly buckling from his audacious declaration. "Why should I listen to what you have to say?"

"Insolent boy!" the Master bellowed, and his eyes flashed a fiery crimson with rage. "Can you not see that I am gaining strength even now? Dare to disobey me, and I will destroy you along with everyone you hold dear! I am quickly learning the ways of your world, and I will take my place as *king* among your kings here."

The sound of the approaching flying monkeys all but drowned them out now.

"Not if I can help it," said Donald.

The Master bared his jagged teeth in a maniacal yellow grimace as he stretched his spindly arms upward toward the sky.

"You will *die*, little boy," he roared with conviction. "This is *most certain!*"

Donald raised the Silver Shoe high above his head and boldly recited the words of the Traveling Spell as a blinding silver light ripped through the forest clearing.

Suddenly he found himself in a dark, confined room. He could hear chaotic screams through a bolted door next to him. Just on the other side of it, crowds of men and women charged up and down the long corridors of the castle, crying out in fear, doing whatever they could to prepare for an imminent attack. Donald paused, letting his eyes adjust to the low light from above. His breathing was heavy and uneven with a rush of excitement flowing through his body. At least he took comfort in knowing the missing Silver Shoe was somewhere inside this room.

He had no idea where to find it, though.

There was a single arched window high up on a facing wall, providing just enough illumination for him to notice the antique oak desk in front of him. His hand probed its surface and bumped into a lamp pedestal. He felt for the switch and flicked it on as soon as his fingers located it.

Donald was shocked at what he saw.

Spread out across the desktop were various newspaper clippings and historical photographs. It was as if someone had been poring over them, minutes before he got there. He spotted his mother's likeness with the headline "Woman Abducted Following Collectibles Show Appearance" as his eyes continued to dart around. He picked up a faded black-and-white snapshot next of a young curly-haired boy standing in front of a modest Midwestern farmhouse with "George Clarke" neatly written in pencil along its bent white border. Then he saw two incredible vintage headlines: "McCollum Girl Found Alive, Search Called Off" and "Oz Author Baum, Dead at 62." On impulse, he set his shoe and the ivory box down, unzipped his jacket, and scooped up the materials, stuffing them with care into an inside pocket. Then he zipped his jacket again for added protection as his eyes continued to scan the room. There were no signs of the missing shoe anywhere.

Suddenly his heart stopped. Donald had found his answer.

He saw a solid iron safe sitting on the floor just behind the desk.

How could he break into it with so little time left? He forced the hopeless question from his mind and began pulling open the desk's drawers, one by one, hunting for any scrap of paper that might have the combination numbers scrawled on it.

He began to panic as his search came to an abrupt end with no luck.

Finally, as a last ditch effort, he scooted around the desk.

Standing in front of the impenetrable safe, he reached down and gently tugged its heavy iron door.

It opened without resistance in his hand.

Zeller had mercifully acted in haste ... for just inside, sitting on a shelf ... was the missing Silver Shoe.

George's heart sank as he watched a handful of loyal henchmen charge into the tower chamber again—this time armed with sleek telescopic rifles. They stood at attention like emotionless wooden soldiers awaiting their orders.

Zeller grabbed one of the rifles for himself and moved to the edge of the window. Leaning out, he observed in horror as the first throng of flying monkeys began their final aggressive descent on the castle.

He gestured for his followers to join him.

"It's a tragedy that it had to come to this," said George, shouting above the roar.

"I quite agree, Mr. Clarke," he replied. "Gentlemen, take aim and do your duty!"

Just then there was an explosive flash of silver light in the center of the room.

"Donny!" yelled George. "Look out, son! They're armed and ready to fire!"

Zeller and his men turned to find the diminutive boy standing in the middle of the chamber, with steadfast composure, holding the ivory box in his hands.

He was wearing both Silver Shoes.

"Forget about the attack and get those shoes!" said Zeller. "Do whatever it takes!"

The men planted their feet, squared off, and aimed their rifles straight at Donald as Ellie let out a scream.

The boy raised one hand in a forceful gesture and stretched it outward.

George winced. "Be careful, son," he muttered under his breath.

"Yaquimna-fantra Lyopmin-oshti Wodefie!" said Donald in a commanding voice.

Right away their rifles burst into a colorful shower of rose petals that fluttered over the marble floor, swirling and scattering in all directions.

The astounded men turned toward Zeller for any explanation or additional guidance as the initial wave of flying monkeys swooped down through the jagged opening and began their assault.

One of the first to arrive landed on Zeller's shoulders and started pulling his hair out, showing no mercy. The attacker smacked him in the face repeatedly as two more monkeys grabbed hold of Zeller's arms and stretched them out sideways in restraint. He wailed in pain as his remaining henchmen—those who hadn't fled from the chamber yet—were tortured and teased in a similar fashion, with sharp kicks, trips, and tugs to their clothing, arms, and legs.

George stood next to the window and peered through it with apprehension. He could hear the cries of terror all around him.

Panic ensued throughout the castle just as soon as the confused inhabitants discovered they were defenseless, robbed of all weapons, while hundreds of Winged Monkeys soared effortlessly over fortress walls and through arched windows, invading and pillaging in massive numbers.

He began to see furniture, rare paintings, sculptures, and other assorted treasures hurled with unreserved glee from the castle's many windows and turrets into the steep valley below.

Then a second wave of monkeys began their descent.

"Run for cover!" shouted George as he returned to the others and stretched his arms wide in an attempt to shield Donald and his parents from the attack.

"There's no need to run," said Donald. "They won't harm us."

George was stunned. "How do you know?"

"Because I asked them not to," said one of the monkeys as he landed next to the group. He scratched his head and flashed a fleeting smile of encouragement.

"*Anirbas,* old pal!" shouted George in relief, "It's good to see you again!"

Their loyal friend nodded and turned toward Donald.

"Did I do well, Master?" he asked with eager anticipation.

"*Master?*" George repeated, completely thrown. "Something's not right here."

"*I* control the flying monkeys now," said Donald. His voice was detached and cold.

George shook his head. "That's not possible—not without the Golden Cap."

"You mean *this?*" said Donald as he reached into his back pocket and removed an odd-looking cap made of gold threads and adorned with precious jewels. "I called for it to come here before I entered this room. It belongs to *me* now."

"You were actually able to transport the Golden Cap so easily?" said George. "The power of the Silver Shoes is immeasurable!"

"They have forever changed the laws of your world," replied Anirbas in agreement. "Logic and doubt are diminished in the presence of imagination and possibility. It's the reversal of everything known. Your entire *civilization* is under siege!"

George watched Zeller with the last of his henchmen as they escaped from the chamber.

"There are a lot of things about these shoes you don't understand," said Donald, who seemed to have the weight of the world on his shoulders just then. "You couldn't possibly understand," he added.

His words hung in the air like an ominous cloud.

"I'm sure of it," said George, trying his best to be cheerful, but there was a strong indication that the floodgates of unseen forces had opened too fast for the boy. Donald was in over his head now, and George could see that he was drowning. "I think you know what needs to be done next, don't you?" added George as he glanced at the others, deciding it was best to move ahead without delay.

"And just what is *that*, Mr. Clarke?" replied a weary Donald. He sounded different, curiously poised—almost like an adult.

"You have the power to free these poor monkeys and send them home again," said George. "You can transport all of them to Oz."

"Yes, I suppose I *could* do that," said Donald, pondering the thought. He turned and walked toward the center of the chamber, then spun back around with an unsettling grin. "You would *like* me to do that, wouldn't you?"

Bill rose to his feet and moved closer to his son, clearly concerned.

George could see the hollow, dark circles forming under the boy's eyes. It was a subtle but distinct shift in his outward appearance.

"Donny, what's the matter? ... Are you okay?" said Bill, but his question received an angry and bitter response.

"I'm fine, Dad. That's what you always want me to say, right? Anything beyond that and you're not particularly interested. It isn't something you'd care to discuss."

"Donny!" shouted Ellie. "I think we've all been through a lot these past few days, and—"

"And the strain is just too much for me?" interrupted the boy, wobbling on his feet as if he were about to lose consciousness. "You have ... *no idea*."

"Something is terribly wrong with Master Donny," announced Anirbas, blinking in fear. "I *tried so* to warn him!"

"What do you mean?" said George. His heart was pounding as he moved closer.

"It's always the same with these shoes," said the monkey. "Each time the dark magic is summoned, a bit of good is taken away in payment ... until all that he once was ... is no more."

Mr. Clarke was overcome.

"I ... I didn't know," he replied. "Donny, the shoes are changing you. It isn't worth it. Take them off before it's too late!"

George moved closer yet again, reaching out in an attempt to touch the boy's shoulder.

"Leave me alone!" said Donald, pulling away from him. "I can handle this!"

He set the ivory box and Golden Cap down on the floor in front of his feet and backed up a few steps. Then he took a deep breath and raised his hands in a grand gesture over his head.

"*Yakimot-barufda Oardita-barufti montren Va nombi Oltah!*" he shouted.

The marble floor beneath them began to shake as the Golden Cap rose slowly into the air. It rotated, over and over, drifting higher into the chamber. Suddenly a bolt of orange lightning exploded outside the tower and an eerie wind picked up, whirling around them.

The cap hovered a dozen feet from the ground, glowing a fiery red.

Then Anirbas began to chatter. He cried out as the entire mass of flying monkeys joined him in a collective chorus of bewilderment and ecstasy. Their jubilant noise echoed throughout the castle and extended far beyond its walls into the valley below.

The Golden Cap burst into a ball of icy blue flames and was consumed in a single, brilliant flash of light.

Donald fell over backwards to the floor. He closed his eyes for a moment, reeling from the intense exertion. After what seemed like an eternity, he rose to his feet again and managed a satisfied but vacant smile.

"The cap is destroyed," he announced in a faint voice. "The Winged Monkeys are free now—*forever.*"

Anirbas flew into the air and circled around the ceiling, screeching with joy. Through the jagged opening, hundreds of flying monkeys could be seen, soaring high in the sky. Some of them shot up into the clouds while others turned somersaults with unbridled delight.

Mr. Clarke and the Gardners gathered by the window to observe this unrestrained celebration of liberty—but after basking in the brief moment of happiness, George turned to Donald and held out his arms in resignation.

"As wonderful as this is, you've got to stop now, Donny. It's much too dangerous. You have no idea where it will end. In fact, none of us do. Please, for your own sake, take off the shoes."

"Keep away from me!" said Donald with a harsh look as he moved toward the center of the room again. "I'm not half finished with them yet."

"No, Mr. Donny!" shouted Anirbas. "Save yourself!"

Donald paused, then stared in defiance at the monkey.

"You want to go home now, don't you? Well, *I* can do that for you! I can do anything. Chris and Jon were right—I'm the most powerful being in the *universe* ... just like they said I would be. Everyone, say good-bye to our dear Anirbas and his flying friends."

Donald let out a disturbing laugh as he stretched his arms wide and closed his eyes. Then he began to recite the ancient, forbidden text once more.

It was all George could do to restrain himself from rushing forward to stop him.

"*Talmini-yohsta Farvi-vogiahn-tay ahk-mah gohl-inoo-ah vosh-koh-ay!*"

"Farewell, Mr. Donny," said Anirbas, and he sniffled with an odd quiver in his voice. "Such a brave boy you are! We thank you so very, very much ...."

George and the Gardners faced their loyal companion one last time and watched him fade slowly into nothingness—and before they could offer any final words of appreciation or affection ...

... he was gone.

"Look outside!" whispered Ellie, gazing in awe through the opening.

They turned just in time to see thousands of flying monkeys vanish from the skies overhead and from their perches in the treetops below, disappearing forever into the turbulent twilight.

A moment later, the wilderness surrounding the castle was silent and peaceful once more.

"Well, that was fun," said Donald with resounding emptiness. His face was hard and sullen as he waited for a reaction from the others. "So ... *what's next?*"

"You must open the ivory box," said George with a steady voice, "read the command written on the piece of paper inside of it, and destroy the Silver Shoes."

"I don't really think I want to do that, *George*," said Donald. Then he let loose with a maniacal yell in open rebellion, followed by a numbing stillness.

After that, he struggled to maintain his composure.

"I'm having a marvelous time, aren't you?" he added as he began to pace back and forth inside the chamber like a caged animal. "It feels wonderful to know that I can *do* things now. All sorts of things. Anyone else? There must be a better idea. Maybe I could destroy this castle and everyone in it. How about that for an impressive trick?"

"Donny?" said Bill, faltering a bit. "It's time to take the shoes off. You've done more than enough with them already. We're very proud of .... *I'm* very proud of what you've—"

Just then the door to the chamber opened and Zeller walked in. He was alone and unarmed. He seemed smaller in stature somehow. His clothes were torn, and his skin was showing the early signs of bruising.

"You're still alive," he said with a hushed voice as he gazed at the group.

"So are you," said George, who didn't see much benefit in hiding his disappointment.

"Pity, isn't it?" added Donald with a sneer.

"We don't have any casualties, extraordinary as it sounds," said Zeller. "Everyone is frightened and kicked around a bit, but no serious injuries have been reported anywhere in the castle."

"Imagine that," said George with an air of disgust. "And you were going to shoot them down."

"I was wrong," he replied, lowering his eyes. "I know that now."

"Do you?" said Donald. "Do you also know it was *wrong* to kidnap my mother and bring her here by force? Can you even begin to imagine how my father and I felt for *days* when we thought we'd never see her again?"

"I acted out of selfishness and greed," said Zeller. "Ever since I can remember, I've been searching and praying for—"

"It's not like you just *stole a piece of candy!*" interrupted Donald, growing angrier by the second. "Come on, Zeller! A much better apology is in order!"

"I'm trying to tell you, I—"

"Too late," said Donald with resolve, and he pointed a condemning finger at his opponent. "I've decided *you* should be the one who is shot down now," he added. "That's what you were planning to do with the Winged Monkeys, right?"

Zeller froze in horror.

"Donny, no!" said Ellie, begging him. "This isn't the answer!"

"Kolmee-nonzat qualin-dab Olmay-estam vomj!" shouted the boy with a satisfied grin, and Owen Zeller began to rise into the air, floating above them in the chamber.

Donald was able to control him with a simple gesture of his hand as Zeller cried out and struggled to break free.

"It seems fair," said Donald, showing no emotion as he continued. "In fact, it makes perfect sense when you think about it."

"Donny, *please!*" said his mother, trying again.

"Now—who has a rifle?" he asked with enthusiasm. "Anyone? Or a handgun perhaps?"

Zeller screamed in terror.

"I can't let you do this!" said Ellie as she ran to the center of the room and stood right under their doomed adversary.

"Out of my way!" said Donald. "I know what I'm doing!"

"No, you *don't*, honey," she replied as she clasped her hands together in a desperate appeal. "You can't go through with it. This isn't *you* talking. Think hard, Donny. You know how wrong this is!"

She reached down and picked up the ivory box, then tugged at its lid, attempting to remove it.

"Leave it alone!" Donald roared.

"It won't come off," she announced as she turned to the others for help. Then she looked at the front of the box and froze. "There's a *keyhole* here," she announced. "This box is locked!"

Donald smirked. "Perfect. It's of no use to us whatsoever—just like our friend Zeller here."

"Donny, listen to me. I'm your *mother,*" she said. "And I have a request to make. I want to see if you can do it."

"I can do *anything,*" he replied.

"All right, then—*show* me, kiddo. Never mind about Zeller. He can't harm us anymore, like you said. I want to see if you can get us all home safely. Please? Send your father and George and the two of us back to our house. Can you do that?"

"Too easy," he answered with a dismissive wave of his hand.

"Oh, yes, Donny," added Bill in support of Ellie's clever suggestion. "We should all go home now. We're tired, and we need to rest. Can you get us all home again?"

"Of course I can," he replied, followed by a short-tempered groan. "You *know* I can. We've done it once, coming the other way."

"I'd love to see what it's like," said Ellie. "I haven't traveled using the shoes yet. Take us home, Donny. It's what we should do now—what we're supposed to do next, right?"

"What we are *supposed* to do," he said, repeating each word with steady importance as he rocked back on his heels just then. "Yes ... right, Mom. This is what we have to do next. ... It was our plan."

Donald recovered his balance and tried to relax. For a second, he seemed to remember himself as he closed his eyes and took a deep breath.

"I ... I think I need to rest now," he added.

"I'm sure you do, son," said George, who smiled at him in an attempt to hide his growing concern. "Everyone, let's join hands with Donny so he can get us home."

"What about ... Mr. Zeller?" said Donald, sounding more like his old self again.

"Let him down," replied George. "As you told us, he's of no use to us anymore, so why bother?"

"True," said Donald, and he blinked in fatigued acceptance.

Then he made a simple downward motion with his hand, and Zeller's pitiful form followed it, settling gently on the floor.

As soon as his feet touched the ground, Zeller ran for the door and slipped through it in silence.

"Take my hand," said Ellie with a hopeful smile as she stood next to Donald.

"Mine, too," added George.

Bill joined them as well, and they all clasped hands together in the center of the chamber.

"Okay, show me how this works!" shouted Ellie, sounding as if she were about to ride a high-speed rollercoaster.

"It's pretty cool, actually," said Donald, smiling to her with faint amusement. "Everybody, hang on tight!"

He closed his eyes and recited the now-familiar Traveling Spell.

"*Mahnk-tanilooqut   Kohlbivyosk   Ahshki-nobkwoeardu-fiostahj!* Shoes, take us home to my house!"

They braced themselves once again as the expected blast of silver light engulfed them.

Chapter Sixteen

AS MUCH AS Ellie had prepared herself, it was still an enormous ordeal to travel halfway around the world in the blink of an eye. She was swallowed up in a cloud of dust now, trying desperately not to choke from it—and as the thick haze began to clear, she could see the others standing with her in the living room.

They appeared to be in shock.

The place was a mess with shards of broken glass, drywall, and planks of wood strewn across the floor in front of the Gardners' large bay window that faced the street. A gaping hole, over a dozen feet in diameter, slashed its way through the center of it.

"Donny?" Ellie called out. "Are you all right?"

She waited in the eerie silence for an answer.

"What do *you* think?" he replied after a long pause.

Donald's voice was soured with resentment—and as the dust settled, it became clear that his situation was getting worse. He looked absolutely frightening now.

"... almost like a corpse," Ellie thought to herself.

It was all she could do keep from crying out in fear as she struggled to stay focused.

"We should try for something bigger now, don't you agree?" said Donald, adopting a mock-formality. "Something *far* more exciting this time."

Then he walked around the room with an air of pretentious authority.

Ellie watched him cross to the bay window and stop. She couldn't believe this was her son.

He stood gazing through the freshly torn opening—his bloodshot eyes observing the row of houses on the opposite side of the street—as the sky above them began to cloud over once more.

A low, rumbling thunder followed, echoing throughout the neighborhood.

"How about opening the box?" said George with a calm smile. "That was part of the plan, too, remember? It was our next step."

Donald snickered. "You don't need *me* to do that," he said, still focused on the neighbors' houses.

Ellie sensed that he was fighting to stay connected to the familiar setting.

"Pick the lock yourself," he added with a grunt. "Better yet, smash it against the wall if you're so curious to see what's inside."

Ellie moved toward the fireplace, cradling the box. She paused, staring down at the intricate, detailed craftsmanship. It was a rare antique, indeed. Then she looked back at the others and saw no hint of an objection, so she turned again with steady resolve, raising it high above her head.

She was a breath away from shattering it against the edge of the stone mantle when all of a sudden she stopped herself.

"No, it isn't possible," she said with a gasp. "It *couldn't* be."

"What's the matter?" said Bill, moving next to her.

She was trembling as she gazed at the small silver key displayed on the mantle with several other objects in her prized collection.

"It's my great-grandmother's starter piece," said Ellie in a hushed voice. "The one she gave me when I was a little girl. That's how she got me interested in collecting silver."

Donald turned to face her.

"That *old key?*" said Bill. "You don't think—"

"I'm not sure," she replied in a daze, "but something tells me this key is going to fit the lock, and I don't know why I know it."

She reached over and removed the shiny heirloom from its place on the mantle, then held it in her shaking hand.

"Okay, give it a try," said George. "What have we got to lose?"

Ellie looked back at him, grateful for his support.

"That doesn't make sense," said Donald, following his remark with a smirk of disapproval. "Why would this key open a box that's been buried in the ground for over a hundred years by L. Frank Baum and Dorothy McCollum?"

Ignoring him, Ellie took a deep breath and inserted the key with ease into the keyhole.

A simple rotation to the left undid the latch ...

... and the box opened up.

The others drew near as she reached her fingers inside and removed a small, brittle, brownish scroll of paper.

She tried very carefully to unfold it ... then to everyone's horror, it crumbled in her hands, leaving nothing but bits of old paper and flakes of dust.

A devastating sense of finality swept over her as she lowered her head and began to cry. Bill took her in his arms and comforted her as Donald let out a troubling laugh.

"So the joke is on *us?*" he said with bitter amusement. "All this excitement and running around the world for *nothing?*"

"Donny, please," said George, begging him. "This is tough on everyone."

"Toughest on *me*, though, right?" he replied, snapping back in anger. "Let's not forget that for one minute!"

After a moment to calm himself, he began to circle the group again, studying each of them as he moved from one person to the next.

"Oh, why such long faces?" he added, pouting with mock pity. "It's the end of the line—is that what you think? Why don't you ask me if I can help you?"

Donald stopped in front of George, and for a split-second, Ellie thought she saw a telling glint in her son's eye—a subtle, playful communication from within.

George nodded, noticing it as well. "You know what needs to be said, *don't* you, Donny?"

Donald leered at him without a response, almost challenging him to continue.

"You've got the words to the spell!" said George. "I didn't think it was possible."

"Yeah, well—I've had a crash course in the dark arts today," replied Donald. "I pick things up quickly."

"All right, *prove* it," said George. "We've got one final request for you to—"

"I'll bet you do," said Donald. "And just why do you think I would want to destroy the shoes *now*, George?"

"Because they're destroying *you*, Donny," he answered gently. "Just like Anirbas said they would. They claim the souls of every living creature who wears them."

"They didn't ruin your precious Dorothy, *did* they?"

"She used them *once* to get home," said George. "She wasn't consumed by their power the way you are—the way others were before you." Then George hesitated as if a new strategy had occurred to him. "Dorothy McCollum was stronger than all of you, I guess."

"Very funny," said Donald, groaning.

"She was able to resist the temptation where others had failed."

"She was a *fool*," said Donald. "She could have had *everything*."

A loud clap of thunder rattled the house just then as the sky began to turn a familiar menacing purple, and the wind picked up around them as well.

"No ..." said George, goading him further. "No, the way I see it, *she* was the one with the most power."

"Careful," said Bill. "You're getting into dangerous territory here."

"*I'd* say you were," added Donald. His skin looked more sallow with each passing minute. "I won't listen to any of this!"

The boy's eyes were glassy and lifeless as he glared at the others with utter contempt.

"Hear me out, Donny," said George, circling the boy this time. "What is the cost of having this power? You don't have *everything* if you sacrifice all that is good about you in exchange for it." Donald studied George's face as he continued. "Our final request," he announced with renewed confidence, "is for Donny here to prove his strength one last time—to show us that he alone has more power than the Silver Shoes. That *he* is in control, not them."

Donald wavered, then closed his eyes.

"I ..." he began slowly, "don't know if—"

"I *believe* in you, Donny," said George. "You've got as much strength inside of you as Dorothy McCollum."

Donald shook his head in resistance. Then he began to shiver.

"I'm ... not sure if I ..." he whispered.

"Deep down you know the truth," George continued, putting his hand on the boy's shoulder to steady him. "You've known it for some time. You have as much power inside you as anyone in your family. Their strength is your strength."

"What are you ... trying to say to me?" Donald replied, faltering a bit.

"Mrs. Gardner, your great-grandmother's maiden name was *Henry,* wasn't it?" said George.

She gasped. "How did you know?"

"Sarah Elizabeth Henry, and her parents were Frank and Emily Henry, right?"

Ellie was speechless but nodded in confirmation.

"What's going on?" said Bill.

At that moment, everything fell into place, and she remembered ... half in a daze, half in a dream.

"She always wanted me to call her *Dottie,*" said Ellie quietly. "It was a secret nickname. I never understood why, when her first name was *Sarah.* ... Sarah Elizabeth Henry. Such a pretty name, isn't it? But when we were alone, that's what I would call her. We talked for hours about her early years on the farm in Kansas ... her favorite scruffy little dog .... She never mentioned his name. Those were the happiest days, she told me. My Great Granny Sarah died when I was very young."

"But not before she gave you the one thing she valued above all else," said George. "She encouraged you to start an antique silver collection by giving you to this key."

Ellie nodded, fighting back her tears.

"Our little Dorothy never gave up hope," said George, struggling with his own emotions. "Even as an elderly woman, nearing the end of her life, she tried every way she could think of to pass her secret desire on to you, to find the lost Silver Shoes of Oz. She believed they would end up in the right hands someday. Donny ... Dorothy McCollum was your great-great grandmother."

Donald didn't move.

He closed his eyes as a single tear rolled down his cheek. Then he unzipped his jacket and reached carefully into its inner pocket. He began to remove several newspaper clippings and photographs.

"I found these lying on an old desk in the castle," he announced.

His voice seemed far away as he spread everything out with meticulous purpose on the table next to the fireplace.

George picked up one of the smaller photos. He was overwhelmed by it as he studied it closely. Then he held it out for the rest of them to see.

"That's *me* when I was a boy on our farm in Missouri," he said. His voice cracked a bit.

Ellie's eyes scanned the headlines announcing her own kidnapping, the frail articles heralding the disappearance of the McCollum girl, and the concentrated effort to find her again. They settled on a late nineteenth-century portrait of a child as Ellie's heart beat faster.

"That's my Great Granny Sarah," she cried out. "I have pictures of her in our family albums. That's her!"

She turned the thick cardboard photo over, and in faded letters, hand-printed in brown ink on the reverse side, was the name:

DOROTHY McCOLLUM

"How can I believe this?" she asked as she began to cry again.

"I have your proof ... from L. Frank Baum," said George. He turned to Donald and Bill. "A copy of his list. I told you both about it in the car. Many names were printed on it. Some well-known, some not, but each has a direct connection to Oz. The name 'Dorothy McCollum' is written in the *margins* next to three other names—Frank Henry, Emily Henry, and Sarah Elizabeth Henry."

"Yes," said Donald, closing his eyes again. "I understand now."

A moment later, he opened them and stared at the others.

Iron determination and abject fear flashed across his face as he looked at each of them one last time. Then he took a deep breath, extended his arms wide, and spoke with transformed energy in a loud, commanding voice ....

"*Elbmatiph-orry Stanshist Ah-may Qenta Orm oh-saykent Ah-stoh!
Elbmatiph-orry Stanshist Ah-may Qenta Orm oh-saykent Ah-stoh!
Elbmatiph-orry ....*"

The Silver Shoes began to glow from within. Red beams of light shot through the ancient markings and stretched across the living room floor, spreading out with increasing intensity.

Everyone backed off and took cover wherever they could as Donald continued to recite the forbidden text with fanatical determination.

Right away the wind whipped around the house in rebellion, slicing through the opening of the bay window as the sky outside shifted to an ominous shade of green.

"*Elbmatiph-orry Stanshist Ah-may Qenta Orm oh-saykent Ah-stoh!
Elbmatiph-orry Stanshist Ah-may Qenta Orm oh-saykent Ah-stoh ....*"

Without warning, there was a violent explosion of light beneath Donald's feet. The house shook from its impact as everyone shielded their eyes to avoid harm.

And when they opened them again ...

... the world around them had changed.

It was peaceful once more. In an instant, the threatening sky had returned to normal.

The Gardners and Mr. Clarke ventured from their temporary shelters to see what had happened.

Donald looked so small as he stood alone in the middle of the room.

The large Persian rug beneath his feet was scorched in a jagged, black circle that radiated outward ...

... but the Silver Shoes of Oz were gone.

He stared with a look of amazement at his plain white socks.

"I did it," he said, gasping for air, followed by an exhausted but satisfied smile. "I was actually able to ...."

Ellie and Bill rushed forward to embrace their son as he collapsed into their open arms and fell unconscious.

Chapter Seventeen

DONALD AWOKE, STARING up at the ceiling. He rubbed his eyes and tried to focus.

Daylight poured through the window from a welcoming morning sun as he lay quiet for a good long while, feeling calm and secure.

He was in his own bed now, safe and sound.

"Donny," whispered his mother. "Are you okay, kiddo?"

His gaze drifted down until he saw her keeping watch over him, sitting in a chair by his feet.

"I guess so," he replied, whispering back. "Yeah, I'm fine," he added after giving it more thought. "How about you?"

There was a lot to be thankful for, he realized.

Ellie smiled at him and sighed. "I'm pretty tired, but I'm doing much better now. You've been unconscious for nearly an hour."

"Thank God you're all right," said Bill, observing them both from across the room.

Donald looked up to see his dad and Mr. Clarke standing in the doorway, grinning from ear to ear with relief.

Then he yawned.

"The shoes—are they gone?" he asked, almost as an afterthought.

"You destroyed them," said Bill. "You saved all of us, Donny. You accomplished more than I ... what I mean is ... that was an *incredible* display of .... oh, George, help me out here, will you?"

Ellie gave her husband a look of encouragement.

"You're doing fine, Bill," she said.

"Donny ..." he continued. Then Bill moved closer to the bed and took a deep breath. "I'm ... so proud that you're my boy."

He leaned down and gave his son a hug.

"Thanks," said Donald, hugging his father back tightly. He closed his eyes and let it sink in. "I remember standing in the living room wearing the shoes," he added, still struggling to recover his memory, "then Mr. Clarke telling us about Dorothy. ... She's *related* to us?"

George nodded. "Your great-great grandmother. I've been talking it over with your mom, and we're not exactly sure how the McCollums escaped from the farmhouse that day, but it seems they ended up living not far from here. Her aunt and uncle assumed false names and pretended to be her parents. Later on, the *Henrys* returned to Kansas and continued their lives under these new identities, guarding their incredible secret for—"

Suddenly the front doorbell chimed.

Everyone froze, not knowing what to do next.

Bill crossed to the window and opened it. He gazed down at the front porch landing.

"Mr. Gardner?" shouted a youthful voice, familiar to him. "You *are* home! See, Chris? I *told* you they were back!"

"That's a pretty big hole you've got in your living room," added Chris, pointing to his left.

"Is Donny home, too?" said Jon.

Donald jumped out of bed and peered over his father's shoulder. He waved to his friends through the window.

"I'm here!" he called out. Then he turned to his dad with mounting excitement. "Can they come up now? Please?"

"Bill ..." said George, drawing an uneasy breath, "I don't think it's wise to—"

"Don't worry, Mr. Clarke," said Donald. "They know all about the shoes. They were with me when I tried the first one on, and they helped me clean up this room after Anirbas broke in here and tried to steal it."

"Do you feel up to having guests so soon?" asked his father.

"You bet I do," he replied. "They're not gonna believe *any* of this!"

"Come on up, fellas," said Bill, waving at them.

A moment later, Donald heard his friends clomping up the stairs.

"I was afraid of this," said George with an anxious look. "We have to be very careful about what we say and who we say it to."

"I understand the need for discretion, of course," said Bill. "We don't want people thinking we're nuts or anything. But the shoes are *gone* now, George. Wasn't that the point?" He put his hand on Mr. Clarke's shoulder in a gesture of support. "You can stop running."

George shrugged. "I'm not so sure about that."

The rest of the morning was spent inside the house. George and Bill found some plywood in the basement and got to work cleaning up the living room and patching the broken window.

Ellie felt rejuvenated and even hopeful again, now that she was back in her own home—and with the reassuring knowledge that her son was going to be all right, she went down to the kitchen and began cooking an enormous breakfast for everyone.

Chris and Jon elected to play hooky from school, but Ellie insisted on phoning their mothers so they wouldn't worry. To her great surprise, neither of them cared all that much. They were so relieved and excited to hear that the Gardners were home safe and sound that they barely took notice of their own sons' truancy.

In fact, both mothers agreed to call the school's office right away and excuse their boys from class for the day.

Jon and Chris sat with Donald in his bedroom for the rest of the morning and listened with increasingly dropped jaws to his incredible story.

Then, shortly after eleven, they heard an unfamiliar car pull into the driveway and turn its engine off.

From his bedroom window, Donald watched in silence with his friends as two strange men stepped out of a blue sedan wearing sunglasses and dark jackets. The men climbed the front steps that lead to the porch landing.

Moments later, the doorbell rang.

By the time the boys made their way to the living room, the strangers were standing with Bill at the front door.

"May we come in?" said one of them, polite but official with his request.

"Sure," said Bill after a hesitation.

Donald could tell that Mr. Clarke was upset by his father's decision to welcome them so casually into the home.

"I'm Agent Stuart Banning," the first man announced. "This is my partner, Agent Denny Lamont. We're with the FBI, special branch."

"We know who you are," said George, "or at least *what* you are."

Banning moved across the room and stopped next to George in recognition.

"I'm sure Mr. Clarke here has filled you in on what we do," he added. "Hello, George. It's an honor to finally meet you."

"I wish I could say the same," he replied.

Banning shrugged. "That's unfortunate. I was hoping you might lose your unwelcoming attitude now that the shoes have been destroyed."

"How did ...? How could you know that?" said Bill, stammering.

"Well, to start with, you're not running away from us," said Lamont.

"No," said Bill. "We're not running anymore."

"Then the need for an escape must no longer exist," said Banning, and he smiled. "Besides, Owen Zeller gave us his full confession. Our European division is still trying to sort through the details, but we are well aware of your intentions."

"Add that to the highly irregular weather reported in this area earlier today," said Lamont, "and the global disturbance that occurred—"

"Global?" Bill interrupted.

"Yes, *global* disturbance," said Lamont with a nod, "that occurred at exactly 7:49 AM, Central Time."

"... I'll even throw in this nice charred spot on your rug—" said Banning with a laugh as he pointed to it.

"... and I think we can pretty much figure out what happened here," finished Lamont.

"What global disturbance?" said George.

"At 7:49 AM, Central Time, all significant weather activity around the world *stopped* for an instant," said Banning. "Now I know that sounds improbable, but all the tornadoes, hurricanes, waterspouts, floods, monsoons, rain, snow, breezes, pressure changes, and anything else you can think of ceased to exist."

"How can that be?" said Bill.

Lamont chuckled. "The weather bureaus are blaming it on a system-wide failure—a glitch in their state-of-the-art instruments. They've done a fine job in covering up a theoretical malfunction."

"But we know better," said Banning, grinning at Donald. "The portals of Oz disappeared at the exact moment those shoes were destroyed."

"It created an unprecedented interruption in both worlds," said Lamont, attempting to explain further. "Only for a millisecond—but it was there just the same."

"So why are you here with us?" asked George. "Just to offer your congratulations?"

"Partially, yes," said Banning, "but you'll be needing help now, and it's in our best interest to assist you. I won't lie about that."

"How do you figure?" said George.

The two agents glanced at each other with raised eyebrows.

"Well, I know you've had a lot on your minds, but I guess I should remind you that you've been national news lately," said Banning. "What do you think will happen when the police and the media find out you're back home, safe and alive?"

"I'm just grateful we got to you first this time," said Lamont. "I don't think our country can handle a news story about the real live magic shoes from Oz, do you?"

Ellie laughed. "Don't be silly. We wouldn't have told the reporters that."

"Exactly what were you planning on telling them, Mrs. Gardner?" said Banning. "Anyone care to share ideas or suggestions? Just where have you people been for the past few days?"

There was an uncomfortable silence as he looked around the room.

"The FBI has arranged to help any interested parties know you've been found and that all is well," he continued. "Don't forget, our branch specializes in this sort of cover-up. Give it a few days, to a week or two, and it'll blow over. The concerned citizens and media will move on to the next sensational story. They always do, given time—but I'm afraid the Gardner family is going to be mini-celebrities for a little while."

"What about George?" said Bill. "No one knows he was involved in this—or even that he's still alive."

Lamont nodded. "Which makes him ideal for us."

"I don't like the sound of that," said George gruffly.

"The FBI has a job waiting for you if you want it, Mr. Clarke," said Banning. "They'll give you anything you ask for. You've already proven your ability to outsmart our brightest and stay one step ahead of them for more than half a century. You would enter in as a top agent."

"I could never work for you," said George, wincing at the thought. "I saw your men at their finest fifty years ago when they caged my friend Kibbero and carted him away. How you could take such a helpless creature ... and torture and test him like—"

"I know where he was taken," said Lamont in a swift response, "and it didn't involve any torturing or testing. Is that what you think?"

"Kibbero became one of our best informants," said Banning. "He lived with our division quite happily for decades, right in our headquarters. He was treated with kindness and respect, teaching all of us the history of Oz."

"The agency built him a huge aviary to fly around in, so he wouldn't be seen by the outside world," added Lamont.

"We knew we could never get him home again without finding a Silver Shoe first," said Banning, "but we gave him a good life. I can assure you of that."

"And when he died?" said George as tears of amazement and relief filled his eyes.

"He never died, George," replied Banning in a gentle voice. "Winged Monkeys live for hundreds of years. He was hoping to be reunited with you. He wanted you to work for us and thought the two of you would make a great team—that is, until early this morning."

George was speechless as the tears began to roll down his cheeks.

"What happened this morning?" said Bill.

"Kibbero started flying around inside his aviary like a wild animal," said Lamont. "He scared his poor caretaker half to death."

"It was the same moment you destroyed the Golden Cap," said Banning.

Donald gasped.

"We know all about the cap now, thanks to Owen Zeller," said Lamont. "But at the time, we were pretty thrown."

"Right after that, you ordered the Winged Monkeys to return to Oz using the Silver Shoes," continued Banning. "Naturally your spell included Kibbero. His caretaker stood by and watched him fade slowly away. He's only now learning that Kibbero is safe with his family and loved ones in Oz—thanks to *you*, Donald."

"Thanks to *all* of you," said Lamont, looking around.

"Now I know why you've been resisting us, George," said Banning. "But there is so much about our work that you don't understand. Many assumptions have been made."

"We'd like to share the truth with you if you're willing," said Lamont.

Mr. Clarke wiped his eyes with the back of his hand.

"And we need your help," added Banning. "I'm not embarrassed to ask for it either."

"But the shoes are gone," said George. "The chase is over, right?"

"For the shoes, yes," said Lamont, slightly puzzled. "I hope that's not all you think we do with our days."

"Hundreds of cases have been solved—even more we're trying to solve right now," said Banning. "I thought you knew that."

"I've known that organizations like yours have been around for a long time," said George with a tentative nod.

"There are *looking glasses* out there, and *rabbit holes*," said Lamont with quiet enticement. "Lost children, lost cities, and civilizations ...."

"... without sickness or suffering or aging," added Banning. "Or rhyme or reason, for that matter. Parallel realities to our own."

"How about it, George?" said Lamont. "Are you interested?"

There was a pause.

"Could I think it over first?" he responded.

"Take all the time you want," said Banning. "You need to rest and stop running. It's been a long time. ... *Too* long," he added, shaking his head. "But if you decide you're ready, we'll be here to answer your questions. You can even come visit our headquarters—"

"People can do that?" interrupted Donald.

Banning laughed. "No, sir, but George Clarke is no ordinary citizen. In fact, he would be the first civilian ever allowed to tour our facility. We think that highly of him."

"I wish I could go, too," said Donald with a shrug. "I'd love to see it."

The agents looked at each other. Then Banning smiled.

"I'm confident in extending the invitation to everyone in this room," he replied. "You can even bring your two friends here."

"Wow, *really?*" said Donald with a gasp. "That's so cool! Maybe we could all go together with Mr. Clarke."

"We might discuss a few current cases if you're ready to help us out," said Lamont.

"I guess I've got a *new* one for you," said Donald gravely.

He moved to the couch, sitting down as it hit him, and he remembered his darkest hour for the first time since awakening.

The agents turned to each other with looks of concern.

"How do you mean?" said Banning.

"It's not over yet," Donald announced with an intense hush. Then he glanced away. A moment later, he continued, looking straight at Banning and Lamont. "I faced him alone in the woods before the Winged Monkeys attacked. I don't even know his name. Anirbas said he was one of the *ancients*. He transported himself from Oz to look for the shoes."

"I had no idea," said George.

"I was by myself when it happened," said Donald. "He lost all of his powers when he got here. I found him reading this huge book. He told me he was learning the ways of our world and he would take his place as *king* among our kings here."

"We've got to report this right away," said Lamont. "And we'll need your help with the details."

"He's still out there," Donald continued. His breathing grew uneasy. "Even now ... I can feel it."

"You can *feel* it?" repeated Bill.

Donald nodded. "He's not a good man. I'm not even sure if he's human. He's been alive for thousands of years, and he's learned ... *so much.*"

"But he doesn't have his powers," said Ellie.

"Not yet," said Banning. "We don't know what's inside that book—or what his plans might be, now that he's trapped in our world."

"Do you think he knows the shoes have been destroyed?" asked Bill.

"Hard to say," replied Lamont.

"They were his, years ago," said Donald. "He knows everything I know from wearing them. Way more, probably. He was tricked into calling on their magic the same way I was—but for a whole lot longer. I think maybe it drove him insane."

"I don't doubt it," said Banning. "I'm sure that's why he's risking everything now to get them back."

Suddenly the doorbell chimed, and everyone froze again.

Donald moved to the edge of the newly-mended window and pushed the drapes aside. He did his best not to be seen.

After a quick look, he turned to face the group.

"There's a white van in our driveway with a big satellite dish on it," said Donald. "I think it's the news."

Banning headed for the stairs.

"Everyone, stay calm," he said. "Nothing at all to worry about—but we'll need you to remain quiet and keep out of sight as much as possible. Lamont and I will take it from here."

The two agents moved to the front door, straightening their ties and smoothing their jackets in preparation.

Clearly routine for them.

There was still much to consider and much to understand for Donald, his parents, and George Clarke.

But now, at least, there was plenty of time to do it.

"No more boring summer vacations—right, kiddo?" said Ellie.

Donald looked up at her and grinned.

He had gotten his wish for a special summer, all right. Even if his tall order had arrived a little late in the year.

Donald had a feeling that his life was going to be filled with special summers from now on.

And falls, and springs, and winters, too.

"*Operation Cover-Up* commences," announced Banning. "Ready?"

His partner responded with an official nod.

It was obvious they had done this many times before.

The two agents turned to face the door and opened it wide with confidence.

ABOUT THE AUTHOR

PAUL MILES SCHNEIDER was born in New York City and raised in Lawrence, Kansas. At various times he has been an actor, writer, composer, singer, and arranger. In 2010, he relocated to the Midwest from Los Angeles, where he spent a decade producing and designing DVD/Blu-ray menus and interactive content for Hollywood films and television shows.

"*Silver Shoes*" is his first novel, and it was selected as a 2010 Kansas Notable Book by the Kansas Center for the Book and the State Library of Kansas. A sequel, "*The Powder of Life,*" was released in 2012. A combined edition of the two books was released in 2013, under the title, "*The Complete, Incomplete Adventures of Donald Gardner and the Silver Shoes.*" His latest book, "*More Than Tongue Can Tell,*" co-authored with Warner Bros. film star Andrea King, was published in 2014.

For more information about Paul and his books, please visit: www.paulmilesschneider.com.

51942081R00158

Made in the USA
San Bernardino, CA
06 August 2017